Gladiator

Anna Hackett

Gladiator

Published by Anna Hackett
Copyright 2016 by Anna Hackett
Cover by Melody Simmons of eBookindiecovers
Edits by Tanya Saari

ISBN (eBook): 978-1-925539-05-9
ISBN (paperback): 978-1-925539-08-0

This book is a work of fiction. All names, characters, places and incidents are either the product of the author's imagination or are used fictitiously. Any resemblance to actual persons, events or places is coincidental. No part of this book may be reproduced, scanned, or distributed in any printed or electronic form.

What readers are saying about Anna's Science Fiction Romance

At Star's End – One of Library Journal's Best E-Original Romances for 2014

Return to Dark Earth – One of Library Journal's Best E-Original Books for 2015 and two-time SFR Galaxy Awards winner

The Phoenix Adventures – SFR Galaxy Award Winner for Most Fun New Series and "Why Isn't This a Movie?" Series

Beneath a Trojan Moon – SFR Galaxy Award Winner and RWAus Ella Award Winner

Hell Squad – Amazon Bestselling Science Fiction Romance Series and SFR Galaxy Award for best Post-Apocalypse for Readers who don't like Post-Apocalypse

The Anomaly Series – #1 Amazon Action Adventure Romance Bestseller

"Like Indiana Jones meets Star Wars. A treasure hunt with a steamy romance." – SFF Dragon, review of *Among Galactic Ruins*

"Strap in, enjoy the heat of romance and the daring of this group of space travellers!" – Di, Top 500 Amazon Reviewer, review of *At Star's End*

"High action and adventure surrounding an impossible treasure hunt kept me reading until late in the night." – Jen, That's What I'm Talking About, review of *Beyond Galaxy's Edge*

"Action, danger, aliens, romance – yup, it's another great book from Anna Hackett!" – Book Gannet Reviews, review of *Hell Squad: Marcus*

Don't miss out! For updates about new releases, action romance info, free books, and other fun stuff, sign up for my VIP mailing list and get your *free box set* containing three action-packed romances.

Visit here to get started:
www.annahackettbooks.com

Chapter One

Just another day at the office.

Harper Adams pulled herself along the outside of the space station module. She could hear her quiet breathing inside her spacesuit, and she easily pulled her weightless body along the slick, white surface of the module. She stopped to check a security panel, ensuring all the systems were running smoothly.

Check. Same as it had been yesterday, and the day before that. But Harper never ever let herself forget that they were six hundred million kilometers away from Earth. That meant they were dependent only on themselves. She tapped some buttons on the security panel before closing the reinforced plastic cover. She liked to dot all her *I*s and cross all her *T*s. She never left anything to chance.

She grabbed the handholds and started pulling herself up over the cylindrical pod to check the panels on the other side. Glancing back behind herself, she caught a beautiful view of the planet below.

Harper stopped and made herself take it all in. The orange, white, and cream bands of Jupiter could take your breath away. Today, she could even see the famous superstorm of the Great Red Spot. She'd been on the Fortuna Research Station for almost eighteen months. That meant, despite the amazing view, she really didn't see it anymore.

She turned her head and looked down the length of the space station. At the end was the giant circular donut that housed the main living quarters and offices. The main ring rotated to provide artificial gravity for the residents. Lying off the center of the ring was the long cylinder of the research facility, and off that cylinder were several modules that housed various scientific labs and storage. At the far end of the station was the docking area for the supply ships that came from Earth every few months.

"Lieutenant Adams? Have you finished those checks?"

Harper heard the calm voice of her fellow space marine and boss, Captain Samantha Santos, through the comm system in her helmet.

"Almost done," Harper answered.

"Take a good look at the botany module. The computer's showing some strange energy spikes, but the scientists in there said everything looks fine. Must be a system malfunction."

Which meant the geek squad engineers were going to have to come in and do some maintenance. "On it."

Harper swung her body around, and went feet-first down the other side of the module. She knew the rest of the security team—all made up of

United Nations Space Marines—would be running similar checks on the other modules across the station. They had a great team to ensure the safety of the hundreds of scientists aboard the station. There was also a dedicated team of engineers that kept the guts of the station running.

She passed a large, solid window into the module, and could see various scientists floating around benches filled with all kinds of plants. They all wore matching gray jumpsuits accented with bright-blue at the collars, that indicated science team. There was a vast mix of scientists and disciplines aboard—biologists, botanists, chemists, astronomers, physicists, medical experts, and the list went on. All of them were conducting experiments, and some were searching for alien life beyond the edge of the solar system. It seemed like every other week, more probes were being sent out to hunt for radio signals or collect samples.

Since humans had perfected large solar sails as a way to safely and quickly propel spacecraft, getting around the solar system had become a lot easier. With radiation pressure exerted by sunlight onto the mirrored sails, they could travel from Earth to Fortuna Station orbiting Jupiter in just a few months. And many of the scientists aboard the station were looking beyond the solar system, planning manned expeditions farther and farther away. Harper wasn't sure they were quite ready for that.

She quickly checked the adjacent control panel. Among all the green lights, she spotted one that was blinking red, and she frowned. They definitely had a problem with the locking system on the exterior door at the end of the module. She activated the small propulsion pack on her spacesuit, and circled around the module. She slowed down as she passed the large, round exterior door at the end of the cylindrical module.

It was all locked into place and looked secure.

As she moved back to the module, she grabbed a handhold and then tapped the small tablet attached to the forearm of her suit. She keyed in a request for maintenance to come and check it.

She looked up and realized she was right near another window. Through the reinforced glass, a pretty, curvy blonde woman looked up and spotted Harper. She smiled and waved. Harper couldn't help but smile and lifted her gloved hand in greeting.

Dr. Regan Forrest was a botanist and a few years younger than Harper. The young woman was so open and friendly, and had befriended Harper from her first day on the station. Harper had never had a lot of friends—mainly because she'd been too busy raising her younger sister and working. She'd never had time for girly nights out or gossip.

But Regan was friendly, smart, and had the heart of a steamroller under her pretty exterior. Harper always had trouble saying no to her. Maybe the woman reminded her a little of Brianna. At the thought of her sister, something twisted painfully in Harper's chest.

Regan floated over to the window and held up a

small tablet. She'd typed in some words.

Cards tonight?

Harper had been teaching Regan how to play poker. The woman was terrible at it, and Harper beat her all the time. But Regan never gave up.

Harper nodded and held up two fingers to indicate a couple of hours. She was off-shift shortly, and then she had a sparring match with Regan's cousin, Rory—one of the station engineers—in the gym. Aurora "Call me Rory or I'll hit you" Fraser had been trained in mixed martial arts, and Harper found the female engineer a hell of a sparring partner. Rory was teaching Harper some martial arts moves and Harper was showing the woman some basic sword moves. Since she was little, Harper had been a keen fencer.

Regan grinned back and nodded. Then the woman's wide smile disappeared. She spun around, and through the glass Harper could see the other scientists all looking around, concerned. One scientist was spinning around, green plants floating in the air around him, along with fat droplets of water and some other green fluid. He'd clearly screwed up and let his experiment get free.

"Lieutenant Adams?" The captain's voice came through her helmet again. "Harper?"

There was a sense of urgency that made Harper's belly tighten. "Go ahead, Captain."

"We have an alarm sounding in the botany module. The computer says there is a risk of decompression."

Dammit. "I just checked the security panels. The

locking mechanism on the exterior door is showing red. I did a visual inspection and it's closed up tight."

"Okay, we talked with the scientist in charge. Looks like one of her team let something loose in there. It isn't dangerous, but it must be messing with the alarm sensors. System's locked them all in there." She made an annoyed sound. "Idiots will have to stay there until engineering can get down there and free them."

Harper studied the room through the glass again. Some of the green liquid had floated over to another bench that contained various frothing cylinders on it. A second later, the cylinders shattered, their contents bubbling upward.

The scientists all moved to the back exit of the module, banging on the locked door. *Damn.* They were trapped.

Harper met Regan's gaze. Her friend's face was pale, and wisps of her blonde hair had escaped her ponytail, floating around her face.

"Captain," Harper said. "Something's wrong. The experiments have overflowed their containment." She could see the scientists were all coughing.

"Engineering is on the way," the captain said.

Harper pushed herself off, flying over the surface of the module. She reached the control panel and saw that several other lights had turned red. They needed to get this under control and they needed to do it now.

"Harper!" The captain's panicked voice.

"Decompression in progress!"

What the hell? The module jerked beneath Harper. She looked up and saw the exterior door blow off, flying away from the station.

Her heart stopped. That meant all the scientists were exposed to the vacuum of space.

Fuck. Harper pushed off again, sending herself flying toward the end of the module. She put her arms by her sides to help increase her speed. Through the window, she saw that most of the scientists had grabbed on to whatever they could hold on to. A few were pulling emergency breathers over their heads.

She reached the end of the pod and saw the damage. There was torn metal where the door had been ripped off. Inside the door, she knew there would be a temporary repair kit containing a sheet of high-tech nano fabric that could be stretched across the opening to reestablish pressure. But it needed to be put in place manually. Harper reached for the latch to release the repair kit.

Suddenly, a slim body shot out of the pod, her arms and legs kicking. Her mouth was wide open in a silent scream.

Regan. Harper didn't let herself think. She turned, pushed off and fired her propulsion system, arrowing after her friend.

"Security Team to the botany module," she yelled through her comm system. "Security Team to botany module. We have decompression. One scientist has been expelled. I'm going after her. I need someone that can help calm the others and get the module sealed again."

"Acknowledged, Lieutenant," Captain Santos answered. "I'm on my way."

Harper focused on reaching Regan. She was gaining on her. She saw that the woman had lost consciousness. She also knew that Regan had only a couple of minutes to survive out here. Harper let her training take over. She tapped the propulsion system controls, trying for more speed, as she maneuvered her way toward Regan.

As she got close, Harper reached out and wrapped her arm around the scientist. "I've got you."

Harper turned, at the same time clipping a safety line to the loops on Regan's jumpsuit. Then, she touched the controls and propelled them straight back towards the module. She kept her friend pulled tightly toward her chest. *Hold on, Regan.*

She was so still. It reminded Harper of holding Brianna's dead body in her arms. Harper's jaw tightened. She wouldn't let Regan die out here. The woman had dreamed of working in space, and worked her entire career to get here, even defying her family. Harper wasn't going to fail her.

As the module got closer, she saw that the security team had arrived. She saw the captain's long, muscled body as she and another man put up the nano fabric.

"Incoming. Keep the door open."

"Can't keep it open much longer, Adams," the captain replied. "Make it snappy."

Harper adjusted her course, and, a second later, she shot through the door with Regan in her arms. Behind her, the captain and another huge security marine, Lieutenant Blaine Strong, pulled the stretchy fabric across the opening.

"Decompression contained," the computer intoned.

Harper released a breath. On the panel beside the door, she saw the lights turning green. The nano fabric wouldn't hold forever, but it would do until they got everyone out of here, and then got a maintenance team in here to fix the door.

"Oxygen levels at required levels," the computer said again.

"Good work, Lieutenant." Captain Sam Santos floated over. She was a tall woman with a strong face and brown hair she kept pulled back in a tight ponytail. She had curves she kept ruthlessly toned, and golden skin she always said was thanks to her Puerto Rican heritage.

"Thanks, Captain." Harper ripped her helmet off and looked down at Regan.

Her blonde hair was a wild tangle, her face was pale and marked by what everyone who worked in space called space hickeys—bruises caused by the skin's small blood vessels bursting when exposed to the vacuum of space. *Please be okay.*

"Here." Blaine appeared, holding a portable breather. The big man was an excellent marine. He was about six foot five with broad shoulders that stretched his spacesuit to the limit. She knew he was a few inches over the height limit for space operations, but he was a damn good marine, which must have gone in his favor. He had dark skin thanks to his African-American father and his handsome face made him popular with the station's single ladies, but mostly he worked and hung out with the other marines.

"Thanks." Harper slipped the clear mask over Regan's mouth.

"Nice work out there." Blaine patted her shoulder. "She's alive because of you."

Suddenly, Regan jerked, pulling in a hard breath.

"You're okay." Harper gripped Regan's shoulder. "Take it easy."

Regan looked around the module, dazed and panicky. Harper watched as Regan caught sight of the fabric stretched across the end of the module, and all the plants floating around inside.

"God," Regan said with a raspy gasp, her breath fogging up the dome of the breather. She shook her head, her gaze moving to Harper. "Thanks, Harper."

"Any time." Harper squeezed her friend's shoulder. "It's what I'm here for."

Regan managed a wan smile. "No, it's just you. You didn't have to fly out into space to rescue me. I'm grateful."

"Come on. We need to get you to the infirmary so they can check you out. Maybe put some cream on your hickeys."

"Hickeys?" Regan touched her face and groaned. "Oh, no. I'm going to get a ribbing."

"And you didn't even get them the pleasurable way."

A faint blush touched Regan's cheeks. "That's right. If I had, at least the ribbing would have been worth it."

With a relieved laugh, Harper looked over at her captain. "I'm going to get Regan to the infirmary."

The other woman nodded. "Good. We'll meet you back at the Security Center."

With a nod, Harper pushed off, keeping one arm around Regan, and they floated into the main part of the science facility. Soon, they moved through the entrance into the central hub of the space station. As the artificial gravity hit, Harper's boots thudded onto the floor. Beside her, Regan almost collapsed.

Harper took most of the woman's weight and helped her down the corridor. They pushed into the infirmary.

A gray-haired, barrel-chested man rushed over. "Decided to take an unscheduled spacewalk, Dr. Forrest?"

Regan smiled weakly. "Yes. Without a spacesuit."

The doctor made a tsking sound and then took her from Harper. "We'll get her all patched up."

Harper nodded. "I'll come and check on you later."

Regan grabbed her hand. "We have a blackjack game scheduled. I'm planning to win back all those chocolates you won off me."

Harper snorted. "You can try." It was good to see

some life back in Regan's blue eyes.

As Harper strode out into the corridor, she ran a hand through her dark hair, tension slowly melting out of her shoulders. She really needed a beer. She tilted her neck one way and then the other, hearing the bones pop.

Just another day at the office. The image of Regan drifting away from the space station burst in her head. Harper released a breath. She was okay. Regan was safe and alive. That was all that mattered.

With a shake of her head, Harper headed toward the Security Center. She needed to debrief with the captain and clock off. Then she could get out of her spacesuit and take the one-minute shower that they were all allotted.

That was the one thing she missed about Earth. Long, hot showers.

And swimming. She'd been a swimmer all her life and there were days she missed slicing through the water.

She walked along a long corridor, meeting a few people—mainly scientists. She reached a spot where there was a long bank of windows that afforded a lovely view of Jupiter, and space beyond it.

Stingy showers and unscheduled spacewalks aside, Harper had zero regrets about coming out into space. There'd been nothing left for her on Earth, and to her surprise, she'd made friends here on Fortuna.

As she stared out into the black, mesmerized by

the twinkle of stars, she caught a small flash of light in the distance. She paused, frowning. What the hell was that?

She stared hard at the spot where she'd seen the flash. Nothing there but the pretty sprinkle of stars. Harper shook her head. Fatigue was playing tricks on her. It had to have just been a weird trick of the lights reflecting off the glass.

Pushing the strange sighting away, she continued on to the Security Center.

Chapter Two

Harper was almost at the Security Center when she heard the click of heels on the metal grate floor behind her. She barely suppressed a grimace and took a deep, bolstering breath. *Great, just great.*

"Lieutenant Adams," said the clipped, icy voice. "I want a report on what happened, and I want it now."

Harper turned and faced Fortuna Station's civilian commander.

Madeline Cochran had been hired by the billion-dollar company that owned Fortuna. The corporate head honcho took uptight to a new level.

Harper eyed the woman's perfect, dark bob that hit bluntly at her jaw, and her sleek, dark-blue suit.

Who the hell packed a power suit for space? "I don't know all the details yet, Ms. Cochran. You'll need to talk to Captain Santos. But whatever the scientists were working on in the module got out of control. It caused the door to blow. Dr. Forrest was expelled from the module, but I retrieved her and brought her back in."

Madeline gave a sharp nod. "I heard the damage is severe."

Harper ignored her. "Everyone else is okay."

The woman tilted her head. "I already knew that, Lieutenant. Maintenance is down there now?"

"Yes."

"The board won't like this. Anything that goes wrong up here is broadcast all around Earth. Stock prices fall."

Harper didn't give a toss about stock prices, and decided it was best not to comment.

Madeline straightened. "I'd prefer we didn't have any more situations like this."

Harper pressed her tongue to her teeth. "You and me both."

Madeline sniffed. "Tell your captain that I'd like a report on my desk by morning, with recommendations on how we can avoid any future situations like this again. And possible ideas for reinforcing the seals on all exterior doors."

There went her plans to relax with a beer. "You're the boss."

"Yes, I am." Madeline strode away.

With relief, Harper slapped her hand against the electronic door lock on the Security Center doors. After it read her palm print, it beeped, and the doors opened.

"Evening, ladies," she called out.

The two men seated at the large control screens both turned around and simultaneously rolled their eyes at her.

"Here's the hero of the hour," a big, African-American man named Jackson said, smiling at her. "Heard you've been busy rescuing wayward scientists." This was from the small, wiry Keane.

Harper went over to the control screen to log off shift. "Well, you know how it is. I can't just sit around here playing computer games all day, like some people."

The security team members were all tight. She liked Jackson and Keane. They'd both been cops before they'd joined the Space Marines.

Both men made dismissive groans at her.

Harper couldn't help but grin. She spotted the captain and Blaine on the other side of the room by the lockers, hanging up their spacesuits.

Sam lifted her head. "You got Dr. Forrest to the infirmary?"

Harper nodded and hung up her helmet on the wall among the neat rows of security spacesuits. She started to unfasten her suit. "Also ran into Ms. Cochran. She wants a report by morning."

Sam's face didn't change but Harper got the impression her captain was mentally rolling her eyes. "I'll take care of it."

Blaine shoved a hand through his dark hair. "I need a beer. Anyone keen to join me at the station bar?"

"Oh, yeah." Harper pushed the top of her suit down.

Sam smiled. "I'm off duty now, too, so count me in. I'm buying."

From the computer console, Jackson called out, "Yes, heroes shouldn't buy their own drinks." He winked at Harper.

She shot him the finger. "Drop it."

Sam turned, her face turning serious. "One other thing, Harper. The ship from Earth will be here in a few hours."

Harper tried not to stiffen. "Yes?"

Her boss' lips tightened. "You've been on base for nearly eighteen months. Saw you weren't down to head out this trip."

"Nope."

"You hit the two-year mark, and they'll force you to go back for some downtime," Sam said.

"I know." Harper would worry about that when she hit the limit. She had plenty of money stashed away, and a neat, tidy little condo in San Diego. She could take a vacation, or just stay at home.

Home. San Diego had never felt like home. It was just convenient to the base. Hell, she wasn't really sure where home was. Maybe it was because she had no one to go home for.

A vacation, then. But the idea of doing nothing but sitting around and sunning herself on the beach gave her the hives.

"What the hell is that?"

The shock in Keane's voice made Harper turn. At the same moment, alarms started blaring throughout the Security Center. The lights dimmed and turned red.

Red alert.

Harper rushed forward, Sam and Blaine by her side. They stared out the main window of the Security Center. It gave a clear view of the main body of the space station, the planet, and the black of space beyond.

But now, something massive was blotting out part of the space beside Jupiter.

It was some sort of...spaceship.

And it wasn't from Earth.

The vessel was a long, cigar shape and covered in enormous spikes. It was black—a deep, unforgiving black that seemed to absorb light. Harper thought she could make out some windows lit with an orange glow from within.

"Alien ship," Keane cried. He tapped wildly at his keyboard and screen.

"Hail it," Sam ordered. "Play them the prerecorded message that says who we are."

With shaking hands, Keane did just that. Jackson was standing, frozen, staring out the window. Blaine was cursing softly, body tense.

"Jackson, open station comms and tell everyone to stay calm," Harper kept her tone sharp and no-nonsense. "We're not sure what we're dealing with yet. We don't need people panicking."

The big man jerked and raced for his computer.

"They're not responding to hails." Then Keane straightened and looked up. "Their technology is too far advanced for me to be sure, but I believe they have weapons locked on us."

Hell. Harper's muscles were tight as a rock. She had a really bad feeling about this. "We need to bring our weapons online."

"Do it," Sam said.

But looking at that ship, Harper knew it wasn't going to be enough. The space station only had basic defensive capabilities.

They had hundreds of innocent people on the station. And no way to protect them.

She stared at the alien ship. The scientists had always gotten excited, talking about the idea of making first contact. But no one had prepared them for this.

"What's that?" Blaine pointed.

Harper strode to the glass and pressed a hand to its cool surface. There was a rain of small objects spraying out of the large ship.

Her chest constricted. They were smaller ships. Headed their way.

"They're firing!" Keane shouted.

There was a flash of light, and then the space station shuddered. Another alarm started screaming, joining the cacophony of sound. Harper gripped the back of Keane's chair to stay on her feet.

"They've taken out our laser array, and we have a breach!"

"Send out a Mayday to Earth and issue an evacuation," Sam yelled. She spun and faced Harper and Blaine. "We need to get our people to the escape pods."

Harper nodded. She knew they had nowhere to go, but they couldn't stay here, and the pods had enough provisions to last until ships from Earth could reach them.

Regan, Rory...Harper thought of her friends, and the other scientists who had to be panicking. All she could do now was help everyone get to the pods.

Sam had turned to the weapons locker. The captain pressed her palm to a lock and keyed in a code. A second later, the doors opened. Laser weapons—everything from shotguns to pistols—were lined up with precision.

The captain grabbed a shotgun, her face grim.

Harper grabbed a laser pistol and checked it. She already had a combat knife strapped to her thigh. She carried it everywhere she went.

Blaine grabbed a combat rifle.

"Go!" Sam yelled.

They spun and slammed out of the Security Center. They split off, running in different directions.

As Harper sprinted through the corridor, she looked out a window, and saw one of the smaller alien ships zip past. It was triangular in shape, black like the mothership, and covered in similar, wicked spikes.

Harper rushed to the window. She saw the ship pull up, the nose lifting until the craft was vertical. Then it attached itself to the side of the space station. She gasped, arching her neck to peer as far as she could at the surface of the station. Lots of the ships were attaching themselves.

She pulled back from the window and kept running. Others were running through the corridor, screaming and crying.

"Get to the escape pods," Harper shouted.

Someone slammed into Harper. She stepped back and saw Madeline Cochran, looking shocked and disheveled. She'd lost her heels and her feet were bare.

"Lieutenant, what the hell is going on?"

"Aliens."

The station commander's eyes went wide. Suddenly, there was a loud clang on the exterior wall beside them. A spray of sparks showered the corridor around them.

A giant, oval patch of metal started to glow, and Harper stared, speechless. With a soft hiss, the metal disintegrated away.

Two giant aliens climbed inside the space station.

Harper whipped out her laser pistol. The newcomers towered over her, almost seven feet tall, and they moved upright, on two bulky legs. They had tough, brown skin, and beneath it, she could see the glow of orange veins. A set of black horns swept back off their heads. God, they looked like demons right from hell.

The closest alien reached out, and swiped up a terrified Madeline with one huge hand, dangling the woman off the ground.

No. This was Harper's space station, her people to protect. She aimed and fired.

The laser bounced harmlessly off the tough skin. The aliens swiveled to look at her, and she saw their faces were dominated by huge, black eyes with no whites. They also had two small tusks coming from their mouths.

She moved forward and kept firing.

Suddenly, one of them moved. She'd made the incorrect assumption that he'd be slow, but he moved fast, his huge fist slamming into her pistol.

Her gun hit the wall with a clang, and before she could process what was happening, a second fist plowed into the side of Harper's head.

The blow was stunning. It slammed her against the glass window, dazing her.

Through the ringing in her head, she watched as the other alien grabbed a fleeing scientist who was running past them. Both aliens started dragging the kicking and screaming women away.

Hell, no. Harper straightened, pushing aside her pain. She ran, leaped into the air, and landed on the back of the closest alien.

As the alien let out a deafening roar, she pulled her knife and slammed it into the back of the creature's neck. It made another ear-splitting cry, dropping the scientist and spinning around.

"Run!" Harper yelled.

The female scientist scrambled backward, and then turned and ran.

Harper yanked her blade out and stabbed again. Orange blood started coming from the wound.

The alien spun and then slammed himself backward into the wall. He had a distinctive white, puckered scar on his cheek, and right now, he looked pissed. Pain shot through Harper, and she dropped her knife. The alien rammed her again, and this time she lost her grip and fell to the floor.

Damn. She'd broken some ribs.

Two huge scaled feet stepped in front of Harper. She heard some guttural grunts and clicks, which she assumed were the aliens' language. Then the alien grabbed her laser pistol and knife. It dropped them right in front of her face and then stepped on them. There was a crunch of metal.

Then the alien grabbed her by the back of her spacesuit and started dragging her forward. Harper twisted and fought, jamming the heels of her boots into the ground.

But the damn alien was strong and just kept towing her like a sack of potatoes.

Then it dragged her through the hole they'd cut in the wall and into its ship.

She was tossed on the floor at the back of the ship. Madeline was already there, sobbing quietly.

Harper pushed up. "Let us go!"

Her captor swung a fist, hitting Harper with another blow to the head. She hit the floor, giant black blotches dancing in front of her eyes.

She couldn't lose consciousness. She had to stay alert. She had to help.

When she managed to look up and focus, she saw the alien was holding a small metallic device in its hand. It touched something and glowing orange bars appeared, surrounding her and the station commander inside a makeshift prison.

"I'm afraid," Madeline said.

Harper was, too, but she wasn't giving in to it. She got one foot beneath her and stood. The alien with the controller smiled, or at least she thought the movement of his ugly mouth was a smile. The twist of his lips made his scar pucker even more.

The giant alien pressed another button on the device. This time, a puff of something blue filled the cell. Harper instantly held her breath.

Beside her, Madeline fell in a sprawl on the floor. Harper felt her lungs start to burn. This was bad. Really bad. She sent her nastiest glare at her alien captor.

His mouth moved again into that creepy smirk.

The pain in her chest was burning now. Dizziness hit her, and she felt the alien watching and waiting. No, she couldn't draw a breath.

But even Harper wasn't strong enough to fight nature. Her oxygen-deprived lungs won the battle, and she gasped in air.

The blue chemical tasted sweet on her tongue. As she fell to the floor, the last thing she saw was her alien captor settling in behind the ship's controls.

Then Harper's eyelids closed, and there was nothing.

Chapter Three

Raiden Tiago spun his short sword and swung it up against the giant axe coming straight toward him.

He ducked and swiveled. His sturdy and very sharp sword easily sliced through the axe handle, sending the axe head to the sand at his feet.

"Curse you to the sand, Raiden. That's the third axe you've ruined this week."

Raiden turned, lowering his sword. "That should encourage you to move faster, Thorin."

His friend, a tall mountain of a man, crossed his massive arms and grunted. "They call you the greatest gladiator in the Kor Magna Arena. I wouldn't want to show you up in front of your fans."

Raiden snorted. He couldn't care less about the cheering fans.

He turned and stared across the small training arena. It was an oval shape, with tiers of seats ringing it. They were currently all empty. On the other side of the arena, his fellow gladiator, Kace, was training some new gladiators with laser nets.

Raiden's senses expanded and he could sense both Kace and Thorin's essences. All Aurelians had this ability, to *feel* what a person was like. To Raiden, Thorin was strength and power, but

Raiden also sensed something darker lurking in his friend. Kace was bright and strong and straight.

Suddenly, there was the roar of a spaceship overhead. Raiden looked up and saw the massive, spike-covered Thraxian ship heading toward the spaceport. The menacing ship reminded Raiden of the achna beasts that had once lived in the forests of his homeworld.

"Fresh blood," Thorin said.

Raiden grunted again, his gut tightening. The Drak-cursed Thraxians were always busy enslaving people or destroying people's lives. He changed his focus to the high walls of the main arena, which towered beyond the walls of the training arena.

Those walls weren't the tallest thing on the desert world of Carthago, but they were the oldest and had the most influence. Tonight, the arena's seats would be filled with screaming fans from all around the galaxy. There was a rhythm to life here on this distant, outer rim planet, and it all revolved around the arena. Gladiators came and went, rose and fell, all on the strength of their sword arm in the arena.

The never-ending parade of ships came in, disgorging new, would-be gladiators. Some were slaves fighting for their freedom, others prisoners of war, some military men in training who came to test their abilities, and a few—the crazy few—were volunteers looking for the fame and fortune associated with the gladiatorial arena.

Over the main arena, the tall, glowing buildings of the District rose up. The sprawling city of Kor

Magna surrounded the arena but the District only catered to all the rabid spectators who came from around the galaxy to watch the fights.

The District catered to their every need and happily took their credits. Whatever vice you wanted, it could be found in the glitz and glamour of the District—gambling, extravagant shows, alcohol, drugs, brothels...the list was endless. Some of the casino owners were as wealthy as the imperators who owned and ran the gladiator houses.

Strobe lights shone into the darkening sky. Raiden guessed that spectators were already trickling into the arena. The corporate sponsors would be sitting in their boxes, wining and dining.

"Big fight tonight."

Raiden nodded at Thorin. "It's always a big fight."

"But tonight the House of Thrax has a new gladiator in the ring."

Just that name was enough to have Raiden's muscles tightening. Thraxians. A bloodthirsty species he hated to the very core. A species that had taken everything from Raiden.

Spinning, he strode over to the weapons rack. He grabbed an oiled cloth and started cleaning his sword.

Unlike most of the other gladiators, he didn't go for high-tech, fancy, or flashy. His weapon was a classic Aurelian short sword. A strong, straight blade forged from the galaxy's strongest metal. As he cleaned it, neon-green inscriptions along the blade gleamed briefly. In a language he'd learned as a child.

As the inscriptions faded, he shoved the sword into the scabbard at his side. The past was the past. It was best to look forward, not back.

"This doesn't look like intense training to me."

The deep voice had Raiden looking up. Galen stood nearby, a long, black cloak falling from his shoulders. He was always dressed in black leathers, ready for a fight, despite the fact he'd long ago given up fighting in the arena to become the Imperator of the House of Galen.

The Kor Magna Arena was comprised of over thirty main gladiator houses. Some had existed for centuries, while others were new and trying to make a name for themselves. Some were aligned to certain species and planets, while others, like the House of Galen, were run by a single imperator.

Instead of swinging a weapon, Galen now owned and trained gladiators for the arena. He was several years older than Raiden, with a weathered, rugged face with a scar crossing his left cheek and a black patch over his left eye. His right eye was like a chip of ice from the frozen mountains of Ixsander, and his dark hair had the faintest touch of silver at his temples. His body was strong and muscled, and Raiden knew that if Galen ever had to pick up a sword again, he'd still be a force to be reckoned with on the sand.

Galen's essence felt like unbending steel, ice and shadows. Raiden wondered if the man ever showed his true self to anyone.

"You're going to look at the new arrivals?" Raiden asked.

Galen nodded. "Word is the Thraxians have been collecting outside of known boundaries."

Raiden frowned. "Where?"

"Apparently they found a wormhole to somewhere uncharted. On the other side of the galaxy."

Raiden raised his brows. It would take hundreds of years to reach that far with conventional singularity drive spaceship engines.

"Found a few new and interesting fighters that they've brought in." Galen shrugged. "I'll take a look and judge for myself."

The Thraxians were the worst of the slavers. They kidnapped anyone and anything that wasn't nailed down, and made a pretty profit selling poor souls at places like Kor Magna. They didn't care if their prisoners were fighters or not. They didn't care if those prisoners died in the gladiatorial ring, or deep in the bowels of some mine, or in the steamy, humid confines of some backbreaking factory.

The options for slaves in most of the known galaxy were all bad. Raiden knew that better than anyone. At least here, at Kor Magna, you had options if you wanted to look for them. He'd come here an angry teenage boy whose entire world had been destroyed. It would've been easy to give up, roll over, die.

But giving up had never been in Raiden's manner.

"Exotic stock, huh?" Thorin set the pieces of his broken axe down on the rack. One of Galen's well-trained support staff would whisk it off to the weapons master, who'd either repair it or melt it down for parts. The House of Galen employed a large number of workers who cleaned, cooked, and did maintenance. "How about you find a few pretty, exotic *female* fighters?" Thorin suggested.

Raiden knew his friend liked strong women in his bed.

"Exotic? Someone different and strange?" The new voice was smooth and deep. Raiden turned his head as Kace joined them. "You think ladies enjoy being called exotic and strange, Thorin?"

The man was one of the newest gladiators in the House of Galen, but he'd quickly made a name for himself. There was no mistaking that the man was military born and bred. With his straight bearing and watchful gaze, it was clear he wasn't a slave. No, Kace was part of his planet's military elite, doing time in the arena to hone his skills.

The man had duty and honor bred into him. He was an excellent, disciplined fighter who went out of his way not to engage smaller, weaker gladiators. Thankfully, the crowd loved Kace's need to protect smaller gladiators.

Kace shook his head. "No wonder you can't keep a woman in your bed longer than one night."

Thorin shrugged. "I have no desire to keep a female." He crossed his arms over his chest. "At least I have them in my bed…yours is always empty."

Kace's face turned blank. "By choice."

Galen's gaze narrowed on Kace. "You've been here long enough to know the way of the arena. The more interesting, the more different, the more crowd-pleasing a gladiator is, the better they do. The better my gladiators do, the better the House of Galen does. The Thraxians have promised a lineup of unique fighters, as well as some never-before-seen beasts. I want to take a look, although we all know the Thraxians are prone to exaggeration." His pale gaze locked on Raiden. "I'd like you to come with me and give me your thoughts."

Raiden nodded. He hated going anywhere near the damn Thraxians, but he knew the real reason Galen wanted his opinion.

Galen turned to the others and jerked his head toward the training rooms. "You'll be pleased to hear I've organized rub downs for you."

Thorin let out a moan. "Yes."

Raiden smiled. They all enjoyed the firm massages from the team of Hermia healers Galen employed. The rub downs loosened up tight muscles and made them forget, for a second, just where they were.

Galen's icy blue gaze leveled on Raiden. "I want you to win the fight tonight. Just do what you usually do and win, but perhaps you could play to the crowd a little bit more."

Thorin snorted. "Galen, how many years have you been telling Raiden to do that? The guy fights and wins. That's it. He doesn't pander to anybody."

A muscle ticked in Galen's jaw. "You could own that arena, if you wanted to."

Raiden stayed silent.

"He already does," Kace said, his expression mild.

"Let's go get that massage." Thorin slapped the younger gladiator on the back, the light shining off the scales that flashed on his arms. Where Raiden was covered in tattoos, Thorin's skin occasionally showed patches of dark scales in the right light. A second later, the scales were gone. Kace's bronze skin had no adornment. He was clean-cut and refused to change that.

Thorin and Kace headed in, and Raiden and Galen fell into step as they left the training arena.

Raiden wondered what they'd find on the Thraxian auction block.

Anything could happen in the arena. On the blood-soaked sand, you could find hope, despair, joy, pain, and—if you were looking for it—something to take all those away.

That's why Raiden fought. To keep the past, the memories, and the pain, at bay.

***

Harper heard noises and raised her head. At least, she tried to. As always, the drugs made her sluggish and slow. She detested it.

She tugged on her wrists and heard her chains clank. Her shoulder was aching from the last time she'd fought her captors.

She gazed around her cell. The floor and walls were a dark brown, made from a tough substance that reminded her of Thraxian skin. Orange lights embedded in the walls gave the place an eerie glow. There was a tiny lavatory tucked at the back, but other than that, there was nothing else in there—no bedding, no entertainment, no chairs.

When she wasn't chained for punishment, she worked through every exercise and sparring routine she knew. She'd lost track of how long she'd been held captive. How long had it been since the attack on the space station? Days, weeks, months? She had no idea what had happened to Fortuna Station, she hadn't seen Madeline after the two of them had been dragged onto this ship. Every day, Harper wondered what had happened to her friends and colleagues, to Regan, Rory, Sam, and Blaine.

After those horrifying early hours, after she'd been stripped, hosed down with some chemical she'd guessed was to decontaminate her from any Earth germs, they'd strapped her down and injected some device into her skin, just below her left ear.

It was both a blessing and a curse, because now she could understand every word her captors had said. A few times, the Thraxians had let her out into a larger exercise room. She'd seen lots of other alien species, all prisoners like her, and the implant had translated their languages for her, as well. Though, the Thraxians never let them talk to each other.

What she hadn't seen were any other humans.

That terrified her. The ship had stopped several times—just like it had now. She recognized when the engines weren't running. She knew they were stopping at distant alien planets, but any wonder at the discovery of new life forms was replaced with horror. She knew now the only reason the Thraxians stopped was to sell and trade their *wares.*

It had been a long time since she'd been let out of her cell. The Thraxians found her...disruptive. She smiled grimly at the thought. Yeah, those alien bastards had learned the hard way that she didn't follow the orders of slavers very well. And she really didn't like being a prisoner.

Harper moved so she could rub her aching shoulder. It might make no sense to fight them—they were bigger and stronger, and she had found no way to escape—but she wasn't taking her slavery lying down.

Suddenly she heard a harsh beep and she stiffened. She knew what was coming next.

Fluid sprayed from the ceiling, spraying down the walls of her cell and saturating her. The simple gray, loose-fitting trousers and shirt she wore got soaked, sticking to her skin. Her hair plastered to her head. It was now several inches longer than it had been on Fortuna.

This was the Thraxian way of bathing prisoners.

A second later, the fluid shut off. She watched the last rivulets stream down the metal floor and disappear into a long, narrow drain in the center of the cell. In the time that took, the high-tech fabric of her clothes was already dry.

Then, she heard the heavy thump of footsteps outside her cell. Harper frowned. They'd obviously landed at a new location. Were they finally going to let her off the ship? Her pulse leaped. God, the chance to breathe some fresh air...

Pity and sorrow rose, filling her throat. She knew she was a long way from Earth. She knew her situation was bad. She was now the property of the Thraxians, fate unknown. She squeezed her eyes closed and took a few deep breaths, pushing the useless emotions away. Okay, so the air wasn't fresh, but it was breathable. They fed and cleaned her. She was alive, and while she was alive, there was hope for getting free and finding a way home.

A light blinked above the doors and they slid open. Two large Thraxians stepped into her cell.

She still thought they looked like demons, with their horns, their tough, dark skin, and the small tusks framing their mouths. But fighting with them so much had told her lots of other things, too.

They obviously had organs close to the skin at their lower backs; they went down easily if struck there. They had weak joints in their arms and knees. And those large, dark eyes were vulnerable.

Harper swallowed a groan. One of the pair had a puckered white scar on his cheek.

Scar Face had been her special tormentor since he'd dragged her off Fortuna. He hit her a little harder, kicked or struck her more often than the other guards. He hadn't forgotten for a moment that she'd stabbed a knife in him on Fortuna.

Right now, he took the opportunity to kick her. She dodged as far as her chains would allow, and only took a glancing blow to her side.

The other alien made a grunting sound, reached down and yanked her to her feet. He undid her chains and held her still, while Scar Face slipped some glowing, flexible cuffs on her wrists. Then one of them jammed an injector against her neck. She felt the sting and hissed.

As they shoved her out of her cell, her head instantly cleared of the drug haze. She wondered where the hell they were. She got the impression the Thraxians stopped at worlds that were hungry for laborers. Was this new world a mining planet, manufacturing world, or—her stomach turned over—a brothel?

A lineup of other aliens had formed in the corridor ahead, and she was unceremoniously shoved to the back of the line.

Every other alien she'd seen towered over her. She was starting to get the impression that humans were very short by galaxy standards. She was tall for a woman, but since her captivity, she felt downright tiny. She didn't like it much.

There were a few hulking brutes at the front of the line, and the tall alien in front of her looked humanoid, although he—or she, it was hard to tell—had a set of small, pretty, glittery wings coming out of his or her back. She'd seen a wide array of alien forms, although she wondered what the scientists would make of the fact that so many of them appeared humanoid, some nearly indistinguishable from humans.

A moment later, there was a loud grunt from behind her, and the prisoners were shoved into motion down the corridor, their footsteps echoing on the floor. Soon, they shuffled out of the prison area and into the main part of the ship.

Here, the floor and walls were the same dark brown as her cell with arched doorways leading into different rooms. The same orange lights ran along the base of the walls to light the way.

The line of prisoners continued to shuffle down corridor after corridor. Scar Face gave her a few hard shoves along the way, but she bit her tongue, and tried to keep her cool. Then they neared a large, arched door that slid open as they got close.

And Harper's heart clenched, filled with a brief flash of hope. For the first time in ages, she stepped outside.

Dry heat hit her in the face, but she didn't care. She moved down the ramp without taking much notice of it. Instead, she lifted her gaze up to the sky and breathed in fresh air. The sky was a faded blue compared to Earth but it was still glorious.

The sun—correct that, suns—were setting. Two big, orange globes, one chasing the other toward the horizon. She blinked at the light as it prickled her eyes and made them water.

They were led off the ramp, and then Harper felt sand crunch beneath her sandaled feet. She felt lighter and realized the planet's gravity must not be quite as strong as Earth's.

"Move," Scar Face said.

They shuffled forward again. Ahead, a huge, circular building rose high above them. Harper arched her head, taking in the cream stone and elegant arches. On the side, she saw neon lights blinking on and off, no doubt advertisements, and strobe lights spearing high into the sky. It reminded her of a football arena on game night.

They were led into a tunnel. Here, the lights were dim and Harper smelled the faint scent of sweat.

"This is bad," the tall alien with the wings murmured.

"It'll be okay," she whispered back.

He shook his head, glancing back over his slim shoulder. "This is Kor Magna on the planet Carthago. It's *not* going to be okay."

"What's Kor Magna?" She kept her voice down, not wanting to attract the attention of their guards.

The winged alien's eyes widened. "You don't know the Kor Magna? Carthago is a lawless, desert, outer-rim world, and it's famous for its arena."

Harper felt her stomach drop. "Arena?"

"Carthago is a gladiator world." The man clutched his hands together, his wings fluttering nervously. "Everyone sold here has to fight for their life in the arena."

Chapter Four

Gladiator world? Harper's stomach did a painful rollover. She had images in her head of Ancient Rome and the bloody horrors of the Colosseum.

But the images scattered as they were led out of the tunnel and into a small courtyard. It had a stone floor and stone benches lined one side of the small space.

Ahead, she saw others gathered. Again, everyone seemed of various humanoid species. Suddenly, Harper remembered Regan's poker night ramblings about what alien life would look like. Most theories held that aliens wouldn't even look anything like us. Apparently, something or someone was responsible for ensuring the varying species of the galaxy looked vaguely familiar. Just another mystery.

She slowed down a little, trying to get a better look at the people. A hard blow slammed into her lower back, causing her to stumble. She spun and crouched, bringing her cuffed hands up. Scar Face was staring at her with that annoying smirk of his.

The bastard enjoyed testing her. After that first scuffle on the space station, she'd also broken his nose within her first few weeks on the ship. He hadn't forgotten that, either.

Another Thraxian guard pushed forward, murmuring to Scar Face. Then Harper was shoved back in line.

They were arranged in a straight row and Harper glanced around, trying to take in more details. It appeared Kor Magna was a strange mix of old and new technology. The walls around them were made from an ancient stone, and sand crunched under her sandals on the stone floor. The small crowd wore a mix of clothes—robes, leathers, jumpsuits. But then she also saw tech she couldn't identify hanging off people's belts—weapons, advanced tablets, and other strange devices.

As her gaze ran over the small crowd, she noted people who looked humanoid, some vaguely reptilian, and one that had two long antennae on his head and multifaceted eyes, which reminded her of an insect.

Then her gaze moved on to two men at the end who looked almost human. They were both big though. Over six and a half feet tall. One looked a little older, with a scarred face, black eye patch, and a dash of silver at his temples. His body was hard and muscled, though, with strong legs covered by dark, leather trousers. He wore a leather top that covered one arm and left the other arm bare, and a black cloak. His cool ice-blue gaze watched the line without a hint of emotion.

Then she looked at the man next to him and everything inside her went still.

He looked like a tattoo-covered, badass god.

He was an inch taller than his friend, wearing the same black leather pants, but his chest was bare except for leather straps that crossed over his skin topped by a burnished gold medallion. The straps held the blood-red cloak that hung down his back. Power radiated off him. She noted the people nearby were watching him with wide, deferential gazes.

Harper's chest tightened a little. There wasn't an ounce of fat on him, and all his muscles and tattoos—and there were a lot of them—were on display. He was made up of defined ridges and hard ropes of muscle, and every inch of them was covered in amazing markings.

The tattoos had all been done in black ink, no color to be seen. His left arm and shoulder were covered in tribal-looking marks and swirls, his right arm was covered in a beautiful script she couldn't read, and down his hard sides, she saw fascinating images. Something in Harper wished she could read the words and images, understand whatever amazing story they told.

Her gaze drifted up his body, and when she reached his rugged face, she stiffened. He was looking at her.

His eyes were deep green in a face that was too hard to be called handsome, but it was commanding. Harper lifted her chin and held his gaze. She was a long way from home, and for the moment a slave, but she wasn't going to act like one.

The winged alien in front of her started to make

a low keening sound. Scar Face moved forward and slammed his baton into the slim alien's back. With a cry, the alien fell to one knee. The baton had torn part of the alien's delicate wing.

As Scar Face lifted his baton again, Harper stepped forward and blocked the hit with her tied hands.

"Enough." She pushed the baton away. "Leave him alone."

Scar Face spun to look at her, his lips pulling back over his tusks. The Thraxians had black teeth, which just added to their scary looks. Harper swallowed. She knew standing up for the alien was going to get her a beating, but at this point, she didn't care. Watching Scar Face, she realized he'd attacked the other man to provoke her.

You want a fight, you bastard? All her emotions bubbled to life inside her. The fear, the loneliness, the pain, the sadness and the anger. It coalesced into one hot ball in her gut. *You got one.* Harper fell into a fighting stance and raised her arms.

Scar Face raised his baton and Harper moved.

She went in low, jamming her elbow into a pressure point on his knee. Over the weeks and months, she'd tested every point on the Thraxian's bodies. She knew there were certain points on their bodies that were hypersensitive. She assumed that nerves were bundled together at these points, and a well-placed blow caused intense pain.

The guard roared and as his knee gave out, Harper slammed her joined hands up, thrusting into his chin. Then she stabbed her fingers at his eyes. He dropped the baton and she caught it before it hit the floor. Straightening, she whirled around and smashed it into his lower back.

Scar Face went down, making a horrible moaning noise. Harper rested the end of the baton at the base of his head—another vulnerable point. He went still, spitting orange blood out of his mouth.

As the other guards rushed toward her, she dropped the baton and held her hands up. It wouldn't stop the beating, but if she fought a group of them, she'd just encourage their anger, and she'd probably end up dead.

She braced herself for the first blow.

"Leave her."

The deep voice made her head snap around. It was the tattooed gladiator.

He was staring at her, like he could see right inside her. Then he glanced at the man with the eye-patch beside him and they shared a nod.

Green eyes came back to her, the intensity of them searing her. "I'll take her."

***

It had been hours since Harper had been shuffled into a bare cell, deep in the bowels of the arena. Or at least she guessed it was the arena. She'd had a bag dropped over her head and had been unceremoniously dragged down here. No one had said a word to her.

The floor was stone and the bars were made of

metal. She wrapped her hands around the cool bars. Above, she could hear the distant roar of a cheering crowd.

It was clear that there was a fight going on in the arena. She wondered how long it would be before she was tossed in the ring and had to fight for her life. Her stomach grumbled, and she leaned her head against the bars.

"I'm so afraid."

The quiet whisper made her turn her head. In the next cell was a man who looked humanoid, except for some ridges running down the side of his neck. He was huge, towering over her. But despite his size, the giant was terrified.

"I can't fight," he said. "I don't know how. I'll die as soon as I step foot in the arena."

"We don't know what's going to happen yet," Harper said.

"We fight for our lives," another rasping voice said. "Or we die."

There was another man in the giant's cell. She remembered him from the lineup. He had the tall, muscled body of a swimmer, and gray skin.

Harper didn't respond to that. Again, she thought of Rome, and fights to the death in front of barbaric emperors.

So many of the scientists on Fortuna had been excited by the prospect of making contact with alien life. To discover all the new technology and wonders in the galaxy.

This was not so wondrous.

Her hands tightened on the bars. *Just take each*

minute at a time. She just needed to survive. Then she'd find a way home...somehow.

She looked at the back of the cell. Her winged friend was huddled in a ball, terrified. The tattooed gladiator and his friend had selected several people from the lineup but Harper couldn't work out their strategy. Some of the men were clearly fighters but—her gaze fell on the winged alien again—some clearly weren't.

"What's your name?" she asked the big alien.

"Ram. And this is Artus." He nodded at the gray-skinned man.

She saw the winged man alien was looking at her.

"I'm Pax," he said in a gentle voice.

"And I'm Harper. All we have to do is take each day at a time." She saw them all watching her, hope in their eyes. "Be smart, watch and learn, and eventually, we'll get a chance to escape."

More wild cheering from the crowds echoed through the cells, and then it slowly died down. She tilted her head, wondering who had died and who had won, simply for the enjoyment of the teeming masses.

Minutes later, heavy footsteps echoed outside the cells, and the gladiator with the eye patch appeared. His other eye looked like a chip of ice, and something told her that despite only one eye, this man didn't miss anything.

"I'm sorry to keep you waiting," he said. "I want to welcome you to the House of Galen."

"Who are you?" Harper asked.

The man's icy gaze moved to her. "I am Galen. I am imperator of this house, and your new owner."

"So, you're a slaver and we're slaves."

The man ignored her and moved along the cells, looking at all the occupants. Then he waved to another guard he had standing nearby. "This is simply a holding cell. We will now take you to your permanent residence. Your new home." He shot them one more hard stare. "The more you embrace your fate and follow my rules, the easier things will be."

When her cell door was opened, Harper stepped out into the corridor. "I am not a slave. I was abducted. I am not going to 'embrace my fate.'"

Galen moved closer, holding something in his hand. Before she knew what he had planned, he slipped a bracelet on her wrist and snapped it shut.

"What the hell?" She lifted her arm, studying the slim black band. It was made from some sort of molded plastic. She saw the guard fitting the other prisoners with the same devices.

"Insurance," Galen said. "It's embedded with a small explosive. If any of you leave the outer boundary of the arena, it will detonate."

Dammit. Harper swallowed her curse. She saw Galen watching her, and refused to give him a reaction. "You are slaver scum."

Galen spun and the guard nudged them all to follow. With the other prisoners, she followed the man down a tunnel. They moved through various tunnels, before Galen approached a large, arched doorway with huge, beaten-metal doors. Branded on the doors was the profile of a gladiator with an ornate helmet.

The doors opened and they stepped inside.

There was a large, open space. The stone floor was swept clean, and there was no furniture, except for red-and-gray wall hangings with the same gladiator head motif as on the door. One side of the room was lined with doors, and the other with cells.

A sense of helplessness washed over Harper. God, she wished she was back on Fortuna, sparring with Rory in the gym, or beating Regan at cards.

The guard opened the first cell, ushering two prisoners inside. At least the cells were furnished, with narrow bunks with folded blankets on them, and a table and chairs. There was a small door at the back of each cell she guessed led to a bathroom.

The cell door was slammed shut, the metallic sound echoing in Harper's ears. The next cell was opened, and Ram and Artus were urged inside.

Harper was led down to another cell, and the guard fitted a key into the lock. The key looked old-fashioned to her, but then she heard something beep, and knew that the locks themselves were high-tech.

"These are also temporary cells," Galen said. His gaze moved over them all. "Tomorrow, you will face your initiation fight for us to gauge your potential."

Pax whimpered from the neighboring cell.

Galen's face stayed impassive. "Get some rest."

Yeah, right. Harper fiddled with the band on her wrist.

Suddenly, she heard the echo of male voices. They sounded happy, cheering and calling out to each other.

Harper turned, and her eyes widened. Three huge gladiators stepped into the room. Their bare chests were covered in smears of blood.

A huge mountain of an alien was on the left, cheering as he held an enormous axe clutched in an equally huge fist in the air. His dark hair was cut very short, and as he moved, she thought she saw the glimmer of scales on his shoulders. She blinked and then they were gone.

The gladiator on the right was all bronze skin, with an exquisitely crafted leather guard covering his right shoulder and arm. He had a handsome face and thick brown hair, and was smiling at the bigger man.

The titter of feminine laughter brought her gaze straight to the gladiator in the middle. It was the tattooed man from the lineup. His tattoos gleamed from a sheen of perspiration—at least, the ones that weren't covered in blood. His red cape contrasted with his gleaming skin, and two scantily-clad women were under his arms, clinging to him. They were looking up at him adoringly. One was giggling while the other was shooting him a sultry look. They were both beautiful with long, curved bodies.

"My champions are back," Galen said. "Time to celebrate." He gestured for Harper to enter the cell.

She moved inside and looked back through the bars. She saw one of the women sliding her body against the tattooed gladiator, while the other woman was kissing the side of his neck.

She looked at his face and his gaze locked with hers. Even across the space, she felt the power of it.

Giggling broke the spell, and, drawing in a deep breath, Harper pulled herself back into the shadows of her cell and watched the gladiators disappear through a doorway.

She eyed the narrow bunks on the other side of the cell, and noted that one was occupied.

But it didn't matter. Harper had never felt so alone in her entire life.

Soon, silence fell around them. There was a faint glow of light from outside the cell but mostly it was all shadows. Harper sat down and tested the explosive band. It was made from a tough substance she couldn't break. With a huff, she sat back. Maybe it wasn't really explosive. Maybe it was just a bluff to keep them in line.

Either way, Harper decided she wasn't staying. She was going to get back to the spaceport and find a way back to Earth.

She moved to the lock, running her fingers over it.

"What are you doing?"

She lifted her head. Pax was watching her through the bars, his undamaged wing fluttering nervously. "I'm not staying." She was pretty sure she could pick this lock if she could find something long and thin. She eyed the bunk and the metal wire holding it together, then looked back at the man. "I'm going to escape."

Chapter Five

Raiden swirled the ice and Canellian whisky around his glass. He listened to the husky laughter from the two women he'd passed off onto Thorin. His friend had been happy to oblige. They were sprawled with Thorin on a large couch in the living area reserved for the House of Galen's highest ranking gladiators.

The rest of the gladiators Raiden called friends were dotted around the room. Kace was talking with his fight partner, the tall, lean, and lethal Saff, with her dark, gleaming skin.

The other fighting pair in the room appeared mismatched at first, but were deadly on the sand. Tall and damn-near elegant Lore was a showman at heart. He had long, tawny hair that brushed his shoulders and a long-boned face. His eyes were a shifting silver-gray. Lore came from a world where illusion was prized and he mixed his tricks with his skill in the arena. His fight partner, Nero, was as big as Thorin, had tattoos to rival Raiden's, a face no one would accuse of being handsome, and only spoke when it suited him.

Female laughter drew his gaze back to Thorin and the flutterers. Often, Raiden liked to burn off the residual high of a fight with a woman. He liked their softness to his hardness. The little sighs and moans they made. He loved to plow himself between their velvety thighs. He wasn't averse to bringing a woman back to his room when it suited him. Thorin, on the other hand, liked a strong woman and a hard fuck, sometimes against the wall of the tunnels as soon as the fight finished. He never turned down sex.

But tonight, Raiden felt restless.

Thorin was giving a play-by-play account of their fight. "And when Raiden slammed that new guy from the House of Thrax headfirst into the sand—" Thorin clapped his big hands together "—that was the best bit of the night. That, and the look on the Thraxian imperator's face."

Raiden grunted. He wasn't really listening, and couldn't care less about the Imperator of the House of Thrax. Hatred burned inside him. There was one Thraxian he hated more than all of them, although in all his years on Carthago, the man had rarely stepped foot here.

"No," Kace said from nearby. "The best bit was when Raiden ran his sword through the shoulder of the Thraxian champion."

Thorin wasn't finished. "Or maybe the best bit was when I put on a dress and paraded around the arena."

Raiden swirled his drink again. "What color was the dress?"

"So you are listening to me." Thorin stroked a large hand down one of the women's arms. "What's with you? You won tonight, but you were…distracted. And then you handed these two delectable beauties off to me for the evening." Thorin grinned at the ladies. "Your loss, my friend."

Raiden moved over to the window. Beyond, he saw the bright lights of the District. If he wanted, he knew he could head into the city to play a high-stakes game of *Jaack* or a back-street fighting match. Or he could visit Lady Charliza's House of Pleasure—the most exclusive collection of pleasure workers in the system.

Instead, he thought of steady blue eyes looking at him from between cell bars.

"Well done this evening." Galen moved up beside him. "The House of Thrax is not pleased by their loss."

Raiden lifted his glass. Making the Thraxians mad was definitely something to drink to.

Galen studied him before lifting a bottle of whisky and topping up Raiden's glass. Here, in the inner circle of the House of Galen, they could all be themselves. Outside, Galen was the imperator and they were all his gladiators. Back here, away from prying eyes, they were friends, with a long, dark history.

Nothing was ever what it seemed in the Kor Magna Arena. That was the first lesson Raiden had learned as a broken-hearted, seventeen-year-old boy stepping foot on the sand for his first fight.

He pressed his glass to his lips and tossed the last of the fiery whisky back.

"The House of Thrax wants a rematch fight. The day after tomorrow. They're looking for a little payback."

Raiden nodded. They could try.

"They've scheduled a beast fight."

Beast fights always drew the biggest crowds, and the sponsors with the deepest pockets. But every new beast that was tossed in the ring increased the risk of harm to the gladiators. The main types of predators Raiden knew, he understood how they hunted and how to beat them. But the Thraxians loved to find something new and dangerous. Odds were they had some fresh, frightening beasts to let loose in the arena.

"We'll assess the recruits in the morning," Galen said. "We'll take the best of them and put them in the beast fight to test them out."

Raiden felt Galen's gaze on him.

"You going to keep your cool?" his friend asked.

"Always do, G," Raiden answered.

"I know that you and the House of Thrax does not equal cool. But it does seem that you like your vengeance icy cold."

Raiden felt a muscle tick in his jaw. "Don't you want vengeance, too?" He swung around to face Galen. "They destroyed our world, G. They took everything and everyone from us."

Galen's scar whitened. "Making the Thraxians pay won't bring Aurelia back."

Raiden felt that horrible, boiling anger rise. Just hearing the name of their homeworld did that. He pictured that bastard Thraxian commander who'd ordered his family to be executed. Ruthlessly, he suppressed the memories.

"Sometimes I think you hate me as much for saving you, as you hate them for destroying the planet."

Too many confusing emotions threatened. "Don't want to talk about it."

Galen let out a long breath. "No, you never do."

Raiden's gaze snagged on the tattoo covering his forearm. It was the language of Aurelia. An oath, a promise, etched on his very skin the day of his sixteenth birthday. Even now, even though so many years had passed since he'd said it, he could still read the words and recite them in his head.

It was the pledge that he accepted the honor of being his father's heir.

And now it was just a lie.

Raiden turned his head, searching for a distraction. "Who is the female?"

When the damned Thraxians had shuffled in that line of pitiful slaves, at first he'd thought she'd looked small and weak. She was tiny. Next, he'd noticed her smooth curves and even smoother skin.

That was until she'd taken down the guard with a few skilled moves. A Thraxian guard far bigger and stronger than she was. And it was then he'd sensed her essence: pure, clean, and white-hot, threaded with bands of steel.

Thorin's head lifted. "Female?"

Galen shrugged. "I've never seen her exact species before. The Thraxians said one of their ships took a transient wormhole and ended up in uncharted space. On the opposite side of the galaxy."

Someone whistled.

"They found her there," Galen finished.

"Transient wormhole." Kace appeared beside them, his own drink in his hand, and shook his head. "They were lucky to make it back before the wormhole disappeared."

"The Thraxians wouldn't care about losing the odd ship here or there, as long as they find slaves and make their profits," Galen said, an edge in his voice.

"The female is small," Raiden said.

"But she certainly showed some spirit," Galen replied. "I doubt she'll make it through the arena. The initiation fight is in the morning."

The conversation turned back to a recap of the evening's fight. Raiden set his glass down on a side table, and while the others continued to drink and celebrate, he slipped out.

Raiden moved through the now-silent House of Galen. The mid-level ranked gladiators would be in the main dormitory. The lowest ranked gladiators would be in their cells.

Everyone had to prove themselves and their loyalty in the arena before they were awarded the privilege of freedom and more pleasures.

When he moved into the area where the temporary cells for untested new recruits were located, he realized he was looking for the small, fierce female fighter.

He nodded at the guard on duty, then moved

quietly along the cells. All the occupants appeared to be sleeping. When he reached the cell where he'd seen her, he stared through the bars. He could see a blanket-covered lump on one bunk, but the second bunk was empty. He frowned, leaning forward. The person on the bunk was too large to be her.

"Darium." He looked over at the guard. "Where is the small woman?"

The guard moved toward him, frowning. "In her cell."

"Open it," Raiden demanded. For some reason, his pulse was hammering through his veins.

Darium took a moment to open the lock. Raiden strode inside, seeing a large Taurean woman looking up at him. There was no one else in the cell.

"She's gone." Raiden strode out, noting Darium's face turning a shocked shade of gray. Galen didn't tolerate screw ups.

"How did she get out of her cell?" Darium scraped a hand through his hair.

The better question was where the hell had she gone. Suddenly, a figure in the next cell shifted close to the bars. It only took Raiden a second to know this slight, delicate-looking alien was unsuited to the arena. He didn't even need to feel the man's soft, insubstantial essence to confirm it.

"You're looking for Harper?"

Harper. Raiden rolled the name around in his head. It had a strength to it he liked and that suited the woman. "Yes. You know where she went?"

The man nodded, looking torn. "She picked the lock and escaped." He drew in an unsteady breath. "I shouldn't tell you...but I'm afraid for her."

Raiden strode closer and grabbed the bars, watching as the man flinched. "Why? Where did she go?"

The man swallowed. "She said she was going back to the spaceport to find a way back to her planet."

Raiden's eyes widened. "She knows she has an explosive band on her wrist."

"Yes. She said she didn't care. She was no one's slave."

Drak. The little fool.

Darium straightened. "I'll call Galen—"

"Don't bother." Raiden spun, his cloak flaring behind him. "I'll find her."

Moments later, he was out of the House of Galen, striding through the tunnels. He breathed deep, trying to pick up her essence. For him, it was almost like tracking a scent...except he could feel it, not smell it.

There. That clean, hot steel that belonged to Harper.

Raiden broke into a run. She was moving fast. He jogged through the tunnels, cursing when he took a few wrong turns.

The thought of her getting blown to pieces fueled him.

He followed her essence upward. She'd left the

tunnels and gone up to the areas where the arena's spectators gathered before they took their seats before a fight. The long passageway ringed the entire arena and was flanked by open arches. On one side, you could look down on the arena. On the other, you looked out over the city of Kor Magna and the bright lights of the District not far away.

He strode along, her essence getting stronger. If she managed to get out of the arena, the sensors would trigger the explosive…

Then he spotted a small figure in the center of one of the external arches. She gripped the stone in one hand, her gaze fixed downward, her muscles tensing.

Drak! She was going to jump.

Raiden put on a burst of speed. She leaped out…just as he wrapped an arm around her waist and yanked her back.

"Goddammit!" She twisted, fighting him.

They slammed onto the stone floor. "Are you trying to kill yourself?"

He managed to get her under him but a second later, she slammed her knee up, aiming between his legs.

With a vicious curse, he rolled them across the floor. She was fast and driven, fighting to get free of him. Raiden had to use his superior weight and strength to pin her down.

"I don't want to hurt you," he growled.

Finally, he immobilized her beneath him and slammed her arms above her head. She gave another fierce buck, trying to knock him off her and pry her hands loose.

Then she slumped down, her eyes glaring at him in the shadows.

"So, you wish to die?" The thought of her dead made him angry. Why, he didn't know.

"No. I'm leaving. I am not a slave." She spat each word at him like projectiles.

He moved a hand, touching the explosive band. "This is very real, Harper. If you pass the sensors embedded in the outer arena walls, this will blow."

She stilled and swallowed. "You know my name."

"Yes." He tilted his head. "Part of it. Tell me the rest of it."

She turned her head to the side.

His hands tightened on her. "Harper, I am not used to being denied."

"Adams. Harper Adams." She looked up, her eyes defiant.

"My name is Raiden."

"Well, Raiden, I will not be *owned* by anybody."

There were things he wanted to tell her, but like all recruits, she had to be eased into it. "There is more here if you are smart enough to look for it."

"Fuck you," she snapped. "You might enjoy being a slave, but I don't."

There was such a fierce, quiet fire inside her. Raiden stood and yanked her up. He kept her wrists in his hand. "Save your anger for the arena."

She lifted her chin and stayed silent.

"Do you really want to die?" He nodded to the arch and the city lights beyond.

"No. But I'm getting out of here."

"And going where?" he asked quietly.

"Home. I'll find a way back to my planet. Earth."

Earth. Raiden had never heard of it and wasn't surprised knowing how the Thraxians had found her. He lowered his voice and he stroked a thumb over the pulse he felt racing in her wrist. "You can't go home, Harper."

Her lips firmed into a hard line. "I am *not* a slave."

"That's not it. You can gain your freedom, but you'll never be able to go back to Earth."

Her gaze turned sharp as a laser. "What do you mean?"

Damn, he didn't want to be the one to tell her this. "The Thraxian ship that snatched you…it took a wormhole to reach your planet. Earth is on the other side of the galaxy from Carthago and the occupied worlds."

He felt the tension pumping off her. "So? I'll take the wormhole back there."

Raiden dragged in a breath, staring at their joined hands. "It was a transient wormhole, Harper. Completely random. It's closed now."

He felt her go still. So impossibly still. Almost as though she wasn't even breathing.

"I'll…I'll travel the regular way then."

He faced her now, moving closer. "Even in the fastest ship available, it would take you two hundred years."

Her eyes went wide and she shook her head.

Raiden threaded their fingers together, liking

when she gripped his. “I’m sorry. I understand what it’s like to not be able to go home.”

He saw the shock, pain and sadness on her face. She was fighting to control it and comprehend it all. Then her chest heaved. “I’m…alone.”

He couldn’t stop himself. He pulled her in tight to his chest, their joined hands trapped between their bodies. “No.” He felt her shudder against him but she didn’t make a sound as she grieved. “You are not alone, Harper Adams of Earth.”

Chapter Six

Harper was tired.

After Raiden had escorted her back to her cell, she hadn't been able to sleep. She'd felt...empty inside.

There was no way back to Earth.

That thought kept reverberating around her head. Added to that, after so long in her cell on the Thraxian ship, the change of scenery had been unsettling. Whenever she'd managed to drift into a fitful sleep, every sound had woken her. She'd also spent far too much time wondering if Raiden had gone back to the women she'd seen him with earlier in the evening.

Right now, she finished picking at the simple meal that had been delivered to their cells. Everyone was tense, waiting for news of their initiation fight.

"Good morning." Galen appeared. "I hope you slept well."

Harper stared at the imperator and wondered if Raiden had told him of her little escape attempt. She fiddled with the bracelet on her wrist. When the imperator's piercing gaze met hers, she figured he had. She lifted her chin. She didn't care. There was nothing Galen could do to her that could be worse than the Thraxians.

"Today is your initiation fight. It will determine if you join the House of Galen…or not."

Harper wondered what happened if they failed. She glanced around the other cells. Everyone looked nervous, except for a couple of huge men in the last cell. They looked eager.

Then she noticed Pax was missing from his cell. She arched her head, trying to see if he was sitting down.

"Those of you who pass the initiation will be given a medical check and then shown to your quarters. And now you have the honor of meeting two of my best gladiators."

She turned her head and then she saw *him*.

Raiden strode toward them, his giant, muscled legs eating up the ground as he moved. Beside him was a female gladiator. They made a hell of a pair. The big, rugged man with the bronze skin, tattoos, and muscles, and the tall, toned female gladiator with the gorgeous dark skin. Her long black hair reached her waist and was a mass of small braids.

Galen waved a hand at the pair. "I give you Saff Essikani, the best net fighter in the arena."

The woman gave them a nod.

"And you also have the honor of meeting the champion of the Kor Magna Arena," Galen announced.

Harper saw a muscle tick in Raiden's jaw.

"A gladiator with more wins than any other fighter in the history of the arena."

Harper felt a cool chill slip down her spine, while the other recruits all murmured excitedly. Raiden crossed his arms, his green gaze moving over them all until it reached her. He stared at her.

"I give you Raiden Tiago," Galen said. "The greatest gladiator of Kor Magna and the planet of Carthago."

Saff was grinning at Raiden as he stepped forward. His arms flexed, drawing Harper's gaze to his tattoos.

"You are now taking the first steps to becoming House of Galen."

All the recruits went quiet.

"As Galen said, I am Raiden. One of the best gladiators in the arena."

Harper didn't get the idea that he was trying to impress them or puff up his own ego. He was just telling them a fact.

"I don't know your backgrounds. I don't know where you came from or what choices you had or didn't have…but none of it matters." His green gaze bored into Harper. "You are now gladiators, and you are here to fight in the arena. That is now your life."

Harper took a half step forward. "So we just go out there and die on the sand for the gory entertainment of a bloodthirsty crowd."

Something flickered in his eyes. "You go out there to win. For freedom and honor."

"For money," she countered. "No better than animals to the slaughter."

"Fights to the death are rare."

Harper glanced over at Saff. “They are?”

“Gladiators are a big investment. The house owners have to buy them, train them, feed them.” Saff glanced at Galen. “Isn’t that right, boss?”

Galen’s face was impassive but he nodded. “Each house makes a great deal of money from their gladiators winning fights. Not to mention corporate sponsorship. There’s a lot going on in the arena, and a lot of people are here for different reasons, but I can tell you that killing gladiators isn’t one of them.”

Harper remembered the blood covering Raiden and the others when they’d returned the evening before. “But people must get hurt.”

A small smile flirted on Saff’s lips. “Yes, often. And gruesomely. But only the worst fighters, and thankfully, the houses all invest heavily in the best medical tech.”

Harper nodded. “So the gladiators just get patched up and sent back out again.”

Raiden stepped forward. “The better you fight, the easier it is to earn your freedom.” He looked at them all. “Galen calculates the number of fights and wins required for all indentured fighters. After you achieve that, you are granted your freedom.”

Freedom. Harper’s heart clenched. Even if she was free, where the hell would she go?

She looked back at Raiden. The champion of the arena was still here, so Galen would probably make them fight until they were old and gray. “You’re still a slave.”

A grim smile touched his lips. “First rule of the

arena, nothing is ever what it seems."

Saff slapped Raiden's arm. "The crowd loves him too much for him to leave the arena."

So was that what drove this man? Fame and fortune. She felt a bitter stab of disappointment.

He gave her one last hard stare, then looked at the rest of the group. "All of you, line up."

A guard moved down the row of cells, unlocking them.

"We are now going to the training arena for your initiation fight."

As they moved into a line, Harper searched again for Pax. She moved closer to Ram.

"Ram, have you seen Pax?"

The big alien shook his head, his face solemn. "They took him."

"Took him?"

"Get moving." The female gladiator, Saff, waved them on.

As they stepped out into the sunlight, Harper blinked. She felt the warm breeze on her skin and she instantly pictured herself in a pool, body cutting through the water as she swam laps. She snorted mentally. Yeah, like that was going to happen any time soon.

"The rules are simple." Raiden's deep voice rumbled across them. He pointed to the center of the small training arena. A small mound of weapons lay on the sand. "You are to get to that pile of weapons…and fight."

Energy charged through Harper's veins. She saw her fellow prisoners all straighten, some shifting on their feet.

"You do not kill," Raiden said. "You incapacitate. Galen, Saff, and I will be watching. Only the best will become House of Galen." His green gaze met Harper's. "Go!"

***

Raiden watched from the stands as the recruits sprinted across the sand.

There were fifteen of them in total, a mix of species. Every single one of them towered over Harper.

He told himself to stop watching her, but he couldn't drag his eyes away. Her dark hair gleamed with shots of red in the sunlight. As a giant Frystani, one of the first to reach the weapons, swung a giant longsword at her, Raiden fought to stay sitting.

Harper dropped, sliding under the blade, and skidding through the sand. Then she was up, grabbing a pair of short swords from the pile of weapons.

She engaged a shorter, stockier fighter with a long staff. It was clear she was comfortable with the swords, although her fighting style was unique. Raiden watched her moves, fascinated. Despite her size, she was strong, held her swords with ease, and he could see the definition in her arms.

She brought her opponent down and then slammed the hilt of her sword into the man's temple, knocking him out.

Then she turned and a second later was sprinting across the arena. Raiden frowned. What was she doing?

She lunged into a fight to protect a giant Parinthian man who despite his size, clearly lacked any sort of killer instinct.

"I may have been wrong about the female," Galen said from beside him.

"Her name is Harper." Raiden didn't take his eyes off her. He watched her leap into the air to attack another fighter. He tilted his head. She jumped higher than anyone he'd ever seen.

Saff made an amused noise. "Ooh, don't tell me our champion is enamored by the little fighter." Saff grinned. "Yep, he can't take his eyes off her."

"I'm just curious. I've never seen her species before. She's from a planet called Earth."

His gaze went back to Harper. He watched as she pulled back from her opponent's swing of an axe. She moved fast.

But strength and speed weren't enough in the arena.

Raiden forced himself to assess the other fighters. The two giant aliens, one with scaled skin and the other with hair so long it reached his waist, instantly started fighting. Raiden could see they were both seasoned fighters. These two were arena volunteers, not slaves.

Raiden watched the men fight, cataloging their best moves. The reptilian was clearly better, and soon brought the other man down onto the sand with a hard throw.

He looked back at Harper. She was still fighting, and busy defending the terrified Parinthian. She called out to a gray-skinned man and the two of them moved closer, working together.

"Interesting," Galen murmured.

They were too far to hear Harper's words, but it was clear she was giving the man orders.

"She has military experience," Saff said.

"She reminds me of someone else I know." Galen looked at Raiden. "A young, angry, up-start gladiator who likes giving orders in the arena. And protecting others."

Finally, only Harper and the reptilian were left. Her two friends had dropped their weapons and pulled back.

She stepped up, holding her twin short swords. She didn't look nervous or concerned. Her face was calm and composed.

She had guts and skill, but the reptilian was bigger and more aggressive. Raiden tensed. Rules be damned, he was ready to step in if the larger alien hurt her.

With an intimidating roar, the reptilian moved in. He held a longsword, and had a far longer reach than Harper.

But Harper used her speed and size to easily maneuver around her opponent, ducking his swings. As Raiden watched, she got in close several times, leaving small slashes on the other man's shirt.

The reptilian was getting frustrated.

Raiden watched Harper pull back a few times,

allowing the reptilian to attack first. Raiden wondered what she was doing. Then awareness struck him, and Raiden's breath caught. She was testing her opponent. Finding his weaknesses.

The rest of the recruits were on the sidelines now, hooting and hollering. They'd all expected Harper to go down in the first few minutes.

She went in low, swiping out with one foot, toppling the reptilian like a tower of stones. The reptilian rushed to get back on his feet, and Harper left another neat slice in the man's shirt.

She moved back, bouncing on the balls of her feet, ready and waiting. The woman had a unique and effective style.

Raiden watched again as she moved in under the reptilian's sword arm, leaving the man's shirt sleeve in tatters. If she'd been out to kill, the reptilian would've been dead long ago.

She got in too close, though. That was the only thing that worried Raiden. If things didn't go her way, she was close enough that her opponent could grab her and do damage. In the arena, most gladiators used their weapons and stayed *out* of reach of their opponents.

All of a sudden, Harper leaped into the air, making it look easy. She landed on the reptilian's back, twisted her body weight, and sent the man falling to the sand.

As he hit, she pinned him down, bringing both her swords up, crossed and pressed hard under the reptilian's scaled throat.

The recruits all cheered. Saff shot Raiden a wide

grin. "I like your little fighter, Raiden."

On the sand, the reptilian frowned, but when Harper stood and reached down to give him a hand up, he gave her a small, bemused smile.

Galen nodded. "I think we know which recruits we'll keep and which need to go." He stood. "I'll make arrangements. And the both of you can go down there and test them out a little more."

Raiden nodded, then vaulted himself over the railing. His boots hit the sand and he strode toward the recruits. He heard Saff following him, sensed her sharp, dark essence.

Keeping his gaze trained on Harper, he moved right in front of her. "Well done."

"Thanks."

"Let's see how you do against me."

Her eyes widened. Raiden had a second to mentally curse himself. He hadn't planned to spar with her. He felt Saff watching him with interest, but refused to meet her gaze. She knew he never challenged recruits to a fight.

Harper nodded. "Okay, gladiator."

Again, no fear in her. This woman had been kidnapped, torn from her planet, torn from her side of the galaxy, and tossed into terrible circumstances. Damned if it didn't make Raiden respect her.

He pulled out his short sword. The inscriptions gleamed in the sunlight, and a second later, similar inscriptions glowed on Harper's swords. She blinked as she saw them.

Yes, she'd chosen Aurelian short swords, just

like his. Raiden circled her. He couldn't afford to like Harper. He couldn't afford to like anybody. Life had taught him that everyone you cared for was eventually torn away from you. Everyone he'd ever cared about had died.

Eighteen years in the arena had taught him to care for nothing but his purpose.

"Begin," Saff called out.

Raiden's plan was to disable Harper quickly. But as he closed in, she moved, fast, out of his reach. Their swords clashed a few times, and he saw her struggle under the force of his blows. Then she lunged in close, and scraped her sword against the gauntlet on his forearm. But she was gone again, spinning away before he could make contact with her weapon.

As they danced, metal rang against metal. She was putting a lot of effort into their fight, and he noted with interest that she was stronger than she looked.

At first, their spectators had cheered them on, with hoots and hollers, but as the battle increased in intensity, the sound slowly died down.

Raiden knew he just had to be patient. Soon, she'd get too close, and he could take her.

As the minutes ticked by, he was surprised to find he was breathing more heavily. Damn, she was good. He also had to admit to being slightly distracted by the tantalizing brushes of her strong body against his. It was something he wasn't used to noticing in a fight. She might be strong and toned, but she was also soft and smelled like a woman.

Finally, she did what he'd been waiting for. With another wild leap like she'd done to the reptilian, she landed on his back, her legs clamping onto his sides from behind.

Raiden dropped his sword. He reached back, knocking her swords away, even as he felt the bite of a blade in his bicep. He yanked her over the top of his head.

She didn't cry out, but he heard a startled gasp.

He pulled her close to his chest, ready to set her down on her feet and call the win.

But as her blue gaze met his, she lifted her legs, planted her feet to his chest, and pushed away from him.

Raiden stumbled backward, teetering on the edge of his balance. He dropped her. Harper landed on her feet, then kicked out with a fierce circle of her leg. As he fell back, she leaped on him, slamming him into the sand.

She pressed her knees hard against his neck, the warm core of her close to his face.

"I win." Her face was flushed with her efforts.

"It's not over yet." Raiden rolled. They scuffled through the sand, but this close, he was the strongest.

They ended up with her flat on her back, Raiden's body pressed on top of hers, both of their chests heaving.

This close, he could see a dark ring of deep blue circling her eyes, and the wild, turbulent blue-gray in the middle.

"Get off me," she snapped.

"No one tells me what to do." He tightened his hold on her. "If you let a Thraxian this close in the arena, you'll never win. You'll never be stronger than the other gladiators, but you are fast and stronger than you look. Use that to your advantage."

He saw her eyes darken, and then he pushed to his feet. He liked the feel of her way too much. He had to remind himself that he didn't need a strange, little woman from Earth messing up his life.

He held out a hand.

She studied him for a moment, before putting her hand in his and letting him pull her up.

Raiden pointed to the reptilian, to the long-haired fighter, and then to Harper.

"Tonight, you will watch the House of Galen's best fight in the arena. Watch and learn, because tomorrow, you will fight in the arena. Saff will continue your training today before you are taken for your medical checks. And be careful…she has a bad side you don't want to rile."

Saff shot him a dark look. She didn't like being reminded of the vicious temper she kept on a tight leash.

Raiden glanced at Harper. "Be ready."

Chapter Seven

Harper swung her swords through the air. The twin short swords felt like they'd been made for her. They had straight gleaming blades made of a warm metal that Harper didn't recognize and they were the perfect weight. She often trained with dual swords in her spare time, just for the challenge of it.

She remembered seeing the gleam of inscriptions on them.

And answering inscriptions on Raiden's sword.

But they hadn't glowed again since the initiation fight. She moved through some basic maneuvers. As she warmed up, she felt her skin and muscles loosen, and her blood begin to pump harder. Damn, it was nice to be outside and exercising. And the swords almost felt familiar.

"You move well."

Harper glanced up at the dark-skinned female gladiator. "Thank you."

The woman's smile widened. "I'm Saff."

"Harper."

"I've never seen your species before. You are very small and very smooth."

Harper screwed up her nose. "Where I'm from,

I'm actually tall. I'm from a planet called Earth."

Saff tapped her chin. "Earth. Never heard of it."

"I'm not surprised. We've barely started space travel, and we'd never made contact with an alien species before. Well, before I was taken."

Understanding moved through the female gladiator's dark gaze. "Getting snatched by the Thraxians must have been a shock."

"You could say that." Harper studied the woman's scarred leather gauntlets. "How long have you been in the arena?"

"Seventeen years."

Harper's heart stopped. "Seventeen years. You've been stuck here all that time?"

"Well, I wouldn't say stuck. This is my home."

Harper told herself not to say anything else, but the words tumbled out of her mouth. "And Raiden?"

"He's been here one year longer than I have." Saff put her hands on her hips. "He's of royal blood. A prince."

A prince? Harper blinked. "How did he end up here?"

"His story to tell. Every gladiator has their own sordid story." Something painful flashed in the woman's eyes, then was gone. "Prince Raiden Tiago is the greatest gladiator the Kor Magna Arena has ever seen. Past or present. He's also a decent man. They're hard to find."

Harper smiled. "The same is true on Earth."

Saff winked. "Harper, I think that's true of the entire galaxy."

"So you and Raiden...?"

Saff snorted. "Oh, no. He's like my brother." She waved a hand. "Now, get back to your training."

Harper trained for hours on end, until her muscles were burning from overexertion. She noticed that Pax never appeared and Ram had gone missing now, too. Unease skated through her.

She flicked out her arm, trying to get the mind-control shield Saff had given her to activate.

Nothing happened. She glared at the thick, metallic band circling her wrist and forearm. She'd been told that the thing somehow connected with her thoughts, and with one flick and a thought, the shield would extend.

But she couldn't get the damn thing to work.

God, she was tired. All day she'd trained hard, working with all the unfamiliar weapons, trying to get used to them.

She flipped out her arm again, concentrating her thoughts on that metallic band. *Activate.* She had to admit, knowing there were weapons that could connect with her thoughts freaked her out a little.

Nothing happened. Grinding her teeth, she kicked at the sand.

"The *tarion* requires a finer touch," a deep voice said from behind her.

Great. Harper tried not to stiffen. This was just what she needed. Raiden had clearly been watching her failure.

She glanced over her shoulder. "Oh? You don't strike me as a finer touch kind of guy."

He raised one brow. "I do whatever I need to do in the arena to win."

Now that didn't surprise her.

He moved up behind her, and the next second, his muscled arms wrapped around her. Her pulse leaped, and she took a deep breath, pulling in the scent of healthy perspiration and man. He moved closer, his chest pressing against her back.

No one had held her this close for a very long time. She'd spent so long locked up alone in a cell, she'd forgotten what being close to someone felt like. Her breath hitched. And before her abduction, after Brianna's death, she hadn't let many people this close.

They both stayed there for a second and then his hands slid down along her arms.

"You can't force the *tarion*." He turned her arm over, touching the metal band. "You need to flow with it. The harder you keep trying, the less likely that it will work."

Harper focused. She could do this.

"You need to relax." His breath puffed against her cheek.

Her thoughts scattered. Relax? He was so damn big and intimidating, there was no way she could relax.

"Remember, force won't work here. Relax your muscles."

She released a long breath. Trying to relax with six feet and eight inches of hard man pressed up against her wasn't particularly easy. Especially when that man smelled as good as Raiden did. Her gaze traveled over his tattoos. She'd never been drawn to tattoos before, but Raiden's were so interesting and added to the badass package. Why did the man have to be so sexy?

"Try again," he ordered.

She moved her arm again, flicking it out.

"That's it," he said. "Imagine the shield extending up in front of you."

His deep voice made the image appear in her head, and the next second, the shield activated. It was an oblong rectangle of glowing, blue energy extending from the wristband.

Yes! "I did it." She arched her head back with a smile.

The faintest smile touched his lips. "So you did." His glittering gaze dropped, snagging on her mouth.

Time seemed to freeze. The air between them turned hot.

Then Raiden stepped back a few inches. "Okay, try to activate the shield's weapon now. It's an electrical weapon. It'll shoot out the stream that will stun your enemy."

Right. Weapon. Here to fight, remember?

She did as he asked. A bolt of energy shot out, harmlessly hitting the sand in front of her.

Harper pumped a fist in the air. "Yes."

"We'll make a gladiator out of you yet, Earthian," Raiden said.

"We actually say Earthling."

"That doesn't sound very dignified."

A smile tugged at her lips. "I've always thought the same thing."

"What is Earth like?"

"A lot of water." A pang of longing hit her. "We have everything from icy poles, to deserts, to pristine beaches." She remembered not wanting a beach holiday. "I'd give anything for the chance to wade out into the waves."

He regarded her. "You enjoy swimming."

"I love swimming."

"As do I. My planet was covered in lakes. I grew up swimming."

The pain was buried deep, but she heard it. "Thanks for the help with the *tarion*."

He nodded. "It is part of my role here at the House of Galen."

Harper's smile dissolved. "Of course." She scanned the arena again. "Raiden, two of my fellow prisoners, Pax and Ram, aren't with the group anymore. Can you tell me where they are?"

His face went blank. "They are not your concern."

Her chest constricted. "Where are they?"

"Harper—"

She grabbed his arm, felt the muscles flex under her hand. "What have you done to them?"

He lowered his voice, crowding close to her. "For their benefit, do not ask about them."

What the hell did that mean?

"Okay, everybody." Galen's deep voice echoed across the training arena. "Time for bathing and rub downs, as well as new recruit medical checks. Tonight, the House of Galen's best will fight in the arena. New recruits, you will watch and take note."

Raiden gave Harper a nod, then spun and

walked away. She watched him move across to Saff, Thorin, and a small group of gladiators. Together, they moved inside.

Harper and the other recruits followed. They moved into a large room where narrow benches lined the far wall.

Several people moved around the benches, arranging small bottles of oil. They were all taller than Harper but shorter than the gladiators. They were all very slender, wore simple robes the color of the arena sand, and all looked the same. They had rounded heads with no hair and large green eyes. Harper couldn't tell if they were male or female.

"They're part of the health team," Saff said from behind Harper. "They are the Hermia healers, and have the ability to manipulate biological energy. They have magic fingers, and can sense where your muscles need the most massaging."

"Which are male and which are female?"

Saff smiled. "They are neither. Their species is genderless."

"Genderless?" Harper tried to wrap her head around that. "How do they…?"

"Procreate. Well, they are capable of impregnating themselves when they want to create a child."

Harper watched as the gladiators moved to a room off to the side. Steam was billowing out of it. She stepped inside and watched, a little shocked, as Thorin dropped his leather trousers. He stood there for a second, completely naked, before he stepped under one of the showerheads lining the wall. The floor was a lovely cream tile and on the wall, red and gray tiles formed the helmeted gladiator logo of the House of Galen.

Other naked bodies stepped under the spray. Beside her, Saff started to strip off. Harper's gaze flew straight to Raiden. He reached up and unclipped the straps across his chest. His harness and red cloak fell to the floor.

His hands moved to the fastening of his leather trousers.

Look away, Harper. But she didn't. Her gaze was glued to the gladiator. He was side-on to her, and as he pushed his trousers down, he bared one glorious, hard male flank.

Heaven have mercy. The man was pure muscle, not an inch of fat on him. His tattoos continued down his muscled back and down one leg. And his ass…the man had a perfect ass.

Okay, so maybe her mouth was watering. He stepped under the spray and lifted his face up to the water. She watched as the water cascaded over his body.

Harper heard the sound of a throat clearing, and looked up. Saff was watching her, amusement dancing in her dark eyes.

"You look like you need a cold shower, Harper." Saff finished pulling off her clothes, standing naked and completely unconcerned about it.

Harper was glad everyone else was already in the showers. She slipped her clothes off and moved under the water. God, it felt good. She hadn't had a decent shower for such a long time. It made her long for a pool as well. She'd kill to work out her muscles in a nice, cold pool. But she guessed desert planets didn't have swimming pools.

She used the soap provided and once everyone else had left and climbed onto the benches in the next room, she moved to the final bench.

As the Hermia healer started to massage her back, Harper swallowed a moan. Saff was right, the healers had magic fingers.

"Mistress, my colleague will run a scanner over you as part of your medical check." The healer had a soft voice.

She tried not to tense up. "Okay."

She heard some faint beeps.

"You are in excellent health. We are required to inoculate you against some common diseases. It will only sting a little."

Harper felt a faint sting on the top of her left buttock. She raised her head. "What was that?"

"A small implant," the healer murmured, large eyes patient. "It protects you against many diseases and prevents procreation."

Her gut cramped. "Permanently?"

"No, only until it is removed again."

She relaxed. "Okay."

"Please, allow me to continue your rub down."

She did and once again those firm fingers dug into her sore muscles, easing the ache away.

Instantly, the image of a naked Raiden burned into her brain. She pressed her cheek against the padded bench, willing herself to find some control.

An attraction to a huge, alpha gladiator was

hardly something she needed. She had no idea what she was going to do next, but she wasn't staying. She didn't need a bossy male getting in her way.

Still—she thought of hard, tattooed muscles—that didn't mean she couldn't appreciate what he looked like.

And it didn't mean that she couldn't admit that she was desperately excited to watch him fight tonight.

***

Raiden sliced his sword through the air. As he moved his body through the warmup, the crowd was already cheering.

This was a smaller, private fight, and he knew the corporate sponsors were up in their swanky boxes watching from above. But he barely spared them a glance. They always invited him up for post-fight drinks and other...delights, but he mostly refused. He much preferred an ale with his friends back in their living quarters.

"The House of Zhan-Shi should be an easy fight tonight."

He turned to look at Thorin, who was also going through his warmup exercises. Across the arena, the helmeted Zhan-Shi gladiators were doing the same.

Zhan-Shi were a small, new house who were still building their reputation. But it never paid to underestimate anyone in the arena.

At least they picked good fighters. Raiden's mouth tightened. They had honor, unlike the Thraxians who enjoyed throwing weaker fighters in the ring. Seeing fighters get pummeled pleased the bloodthirsty crowds. Very few died in the arena, but a lot of people got seriously wounded. The Thraxians understood that the more blood and gore that was spilled, the more the crowd paid.

Raiden's jaw tightened. He wouldn't let that stand. He glanced over toward the House of Galen's seats, which were close to the arena floor, and he had no trouble spotting Harper. She was standing, gripping the railing, as she watched the fight preparations.

"You can't take your eyes off our newest female fighter."

Raiden swung his sword again, ignoring Thorin.

"She is intriguing," his friend continued. "So many contradictions. Small and soft. Looks delicate, but is a strong, skilled fighter."

Raiden still didn't respond. He knew from past experience that if you gave Thorin even the smallest gap, he'd burrow right in and extract all your secrets. Instead, Raiden checked the straps crossing his chest, touched the medallion there, then checked the gauntlet covering his sword arm.

"You can admit to liking her—"

"Her name is Harper, and I do not *like* women." Raiden spun and glared at his friend. "I fuck them. End of story."

Thorin raised a brow. "So, you're going to fuck her, then?"

"No." Harper equaled distraction. Raiden never fucked gladiators from his own house. He didn't get attached. Ever.

"So you won't mind if I sample the pretty woman from Earth—"

Raiden landed one hard punch to Thorin's jaw.

The big man fell back a step, and bit off a curse. He rubbed his chin. "Guess you do mind." He turned his head and spat out some blood. When he looked back, he grinned at Raiden.

Drak. He'd fallen right into Thorin's trap. "Eat sand, Thorin."

Thorin slung his axe over his shoulder. "I'm just here to get you to pull your head out of your ass."

"Drop it."

Thorin opened his mouth, proving that he was an idiot, but Saff and Kace appeared.

"You're supposed to fight the rival gladiators, not each other," Kace said dryly.

"Lucky for us, Thorin's jaw is made of stone," Saff said with a smile.

"What he's got is a big mouth," Raiden said.

"I have something else that's big." Thorin grinned. "And Raiden, here, has a big hard-on for our newest female gladiator."

Raiden sent his friend a scathing glare. "Big. Mouth."

Kace held up a hand. He was holding helmets topped with red truska fur. "The sponsors requested helmets at the last minute. As always, we aim to please those who shower us in money. Galen said to make it look good."

Raiden scowled. He hated helmets. They hampered his vision and added weight. He took it and pulled it on, adjusting to his hampered vision. “We always do.”

He saw Lore and Nero striding toward them. With their helmets, fighting leathers and bare chests, they looked imposing. Lore paused and waved to the crowd. Then he lifted a palm and blew what looked like dust off his hand. The dust streamed into the air, twisting and writhing, until it made a shape like the flying dracos beasts of the Dagon System. The spectators screamed their pleasure.

Thorin pulled his helmet on and all his teasing ended. Through the slit in the helmet, Raiden could see his friend’s eyes were hard and focused. Raiden glanced over at Saff and Kace.

“Ready to fight?” Raiden asked.

“For freedom and honor,” Saff called out.

“For freedom and honor,” Thorin, Kace, Lore and Nero said together.

Thorin swung his axe and the six of them moved in a line toward the opposing gladiators.

Raiden felt his blood fire even as his mind cleared, ready for the fight. The crowd cheered, and he knew many were locals, but more came in especially for the fights from all parts of the galaxy. Lured by the thrill of watching man pitted against man, for the chance to see blood spray across the sand.

Then they stayed for all the temptations and vices the Kor Magna District offered them.

A moment later, the fight siren blasted—a long, mournful sound that echoed across the arena.

As the Zhan-Shi gladiators advanced, Raiden turned his head and caught sight of Harper. She was watching him.

He took a breath, then he turned his attention to the approaching gladiators. Time to focus on the fight. But the image of blue-gray eyes stayed in his head, inspiring him to fight harder.

"For the House of Galen," he yelled, charging forward.

Beside him, his team moved with him.

Swords clashed. The distinctive Zhan-Shi battle cry echoed around them. Soon, Raiden lost himself in the fight. For so many years, this had been his haven, his escape. In the middle of the fight, there was no past or future. There was no lost planet and no dead family. There was no pain or sorrow.

There was only the here and now, and a fight for survival.

Raiden spun and slammed his weapon against the shield of one of the Zhan-Shi gladiators. Raiden didn't recognize the guy, and while he had some skill, it wasn't enough. A second later, the gladiator lost his balance and fell on the sand. Raiden sliced his sword across the man's sword arm and left him bleeding.

He turned and saw a gladiator coming in from Thorin's side.

"Thorin," he yelled at his partner.

The big gladiator spun, roaring as he swung his axe. He took down two gladiators.

Raiden fought another gladiator, this one a little better with his sword. Raiden jumped, bringing his weapon down, and sending his opponent to the sand with a spray of blood.

He turned to face the remaining Zhan-Shi gladiator. The young man was practically shaking, his face terrified.

Drak. Raiden switched his grip and slammed the hilt of his sword against the young man's temple. He collapsed without a sound.

Sweat dripping off him, his chest heaving, Raiden looked across the arena. The only gladiators still standing were his friends. Victory for the House of Galen.

He strode across the sand. Thorin fell in beside him, as did the rest of the House of Galen warriors. As they did their lap, the cheering of the crowd got even louder.

As Raiden passed the House of Thrax seats, he saw the stony face of the bastards who ran the house. Raiden raised his sword at the imperator.

His blood was pumping with adrenaline. He always felt like this after winning a fight in the arena. High on the sensations and the mix of essences that battered him from the crowd. He yanked off his helmet.

He stopped below the House of Galen seats.

"Nice work, boys." Saff bumped her shoulders against Raiden and Thorin.

Beside her, Kace nodded. Lore was grinning and Nero was almost smiling. Thorin slapped Raiden on the back.

Raiden glanced over and saw Harper watching him. She was grinning. Without thinking, Raiden stalked toward her. He leaped up, holding the top of the railing, his face level with hers.

"Nice fight, gladiator," she said. "You might want to know that two opposing gladiators just got back up. They're headed this way. That means you aren't done yet, right?"

Raiden didn't even bother glancing back. "Won't take me long to take care of them."

"Arrogant."

"Confident. Wish me luck?"

"You don't need it."

But when she reached out, Raiden went still. She touched the tip of her thumb to his lips, dragging it across.

"You have some blood there." Her voice was husky. "It's gone now." Her eyes met his. "Good luck."

Raiden nipped the soft pad of her thumb, and saw something flare in her eyes. "You're right, I don't need it, but I'll take it from you."

He leaned forward and kissed her.

Drak. Her flavor exploded through him, igniting his blood. Desire was a solid slam into his gut and his kiss turned hard, hungry. She kissed him back—exploring his mouth with eager thrusts of her tongue.

Following the tiniest thread of self-preservation that was drumming through his head, he pulled back. They stared at each other. The crowd was roaring around them, but Raiden didn't pay them any attention.

Then he turned away and leaped back into the arena. He raised his fist to the crowd, and they cheered. He glanced once more at Harper before he moved back to his gladiators.

With Thorin, Saff, and the others flanking him, they strode across the arena to take care of the last of the Zhan-Shi gladiators.

Chapter Eight

"Let's go through them one more time," Saff said.

Harper nodded, trying to quell her nervousness. She stared at the projected images of all the beasts that they might face in the arena tonight.

They'd had a lighter day of training today, to rest up, and Harper had spent most of the day looking at each of the beasts with Saff, Thorin, and Raiden. Her head was ringing with all the strengths and weaknesses they'd drummed into her. Raiden wouldn't let up. He wanted her to remember every little detail and he was being a hard taskmaster.

For the last two hours, they'd been in this large living area that belonged to the high-level gladiators. It was a comfortable space with exposed stone walls. Saff was operating a small computer, projecting images on the wall.

They weren't sure what beasts the Thraxians would throw into the arena, but some of the images were truly horrifying. Some were like nothing she'd ever seen before. One flashed up on the screen. That one looked similar to the big cats on Earth. The next one that flashed up, with green, bumpy skin and standing on two huge feet, that made her think of a troll from some fantasy story.

"This one has very sharp teeth," Saff said.

"And poison," Thorin added cheerfully. "Don't let it bite or drool on you."

Right. Harper had spent the morning practicing with the nets that Saff had told her were good in a beast fight. The nets were great for trapping and slowing down most beasts. But the damn things were tricky. They exploded out of a small egg-shaped device, but you had to have impeccable aim. By the end of the day, she'd gotten better, but she didn't think the net was ever going to be her weapon of choice.

She glanced at the door she knew led down to the gladiators' bedrooms. They all had their own rooms, while she'd been moved into a dormitory with a group of other newer gladiators. She was just damn glad to be out of the cell.

She was waiting for Raiden to return. He'd gone to prepare for the fight.

Images of the fight the night before rushed into her head. His powerful body as he'd fought with deadly power and precision. He'd been unstoppable in the arena and she hadn't been able to take her eyes off him.

And that kiss. A shot of heat arrowed between her legs and she shifted in her seat.

Raiden was rapidly becoming an obsession and Harper had never, ever been obsessed by a man.

"Okay, this is a *raksha*." Saff pointed to the next image. The giant creature looked like a huge gorilla with matted black fur. "Go for the back of the neck.

That's their weak point."

"The neck, right."

"This is a *gallu*. If they get close enough to spit at you, they have a poison that will paralyze you in about twenty seconds. Go for the knees on this one."

"*Gallu*. Don't get in spitting range." Harper had a good memory, but she was never going to remember all of this. "Knees. You know, a few of these resemble animals on Earth. It's funny that so many sentient species I've seen all look similar." She held out her arms. "Two arms, two legs, head, heart—"

Thorin grinned. "Cocks."

Saff slapped the big gladiator in the back of the head. "It's because of the Creators."

Harper blinked. "The Creators?"

Kace leaned forward. "You don't know about the Creators?"

"They were an ancient species who created life in the galaxy," Saff said. "They traveled the galaxy, seeding life on habitable planets. Creating beings in their own likeness."

Wow. That sounded like a lot of myths and legends on Earth. "Where are they now?"

Saff shrugged. "No one knows. They left nothing behind but the species they created. This was millennia ago. People are always peddling Creator artifacts but ninety-nine percent of them are fake."

Fascinating. Behind her, Harper heard a door open. She looked over her shoulder and saw Raiden stride in, his red cloak flaring out behind him. He'd rubbed some sort of oil into his chest, which made his tattoos gleam in the light. Right now, he looked like the prince they said he'd been. His rugged jaw was set, his green eyes on her.

Damn the man for being so good looking.

She was dimly aware of the other gladiators moving away to finish preparations for the battle. She pressed her hands to the new leather trousers and vest she wore. Saff had brought them for her, along with beautiful leather gauntlets. They felt stiff, but she knew over time they would mold to her shape.

"Ready?" he asked.

She took in a deep breath. "As ready as I'll ever be."

He stopped close by, heat pouring off him. "You'll do fine, Harper. I've seen your steely will and your skill."

She didn't want to think of the fight, not yet. "Raiden, I want to know what happened to Ram and Pax, the aliens I was with when I first arrived."

His face went blank. "Focus on the fight."

Dammit, her instincts were screaming at her. Raiden was hiding something. She didn't want to believe he was bad, but she'd heard whispers among the recruits of the weak and poor fighters who disappeared from the House of Galen.

"Are they dead?" she asked baldly.

He leaned in close. "You think I'm a killer?"

His tone was a lethal whisper. "Yes. I think you're capable of killing, but I don't have you worked out yet." She wanted to believe he was good, but she worried she was blinded by his rockstar status.

"Ask me a question, then," he suggested. "Not about your friends. Something to help you learn more about me."

"Were you really a prince?"

A muscle ticked in his jaw. "That was a lifetime ago."

So now he was just a prince of the arena. "You told me you couldn't go home, like me."

"That's right."

"It hurts," she murmured. "Knowing I'll never step foot on Earth again."

"Is there someone waiting for you at home?" His voice darkened.

She shook her head and thought of her sister. "No one. But home is home."

Raiden reached out, tucking a strand of her hair behind her ear. "Home is where you make it, Harper. My home was completely destroyed."

She gasped. "Your entire planet."

"Yes." A hard word.

"Raiden, I'm so sorry."

That muscle ticked again. "It happened a long time ago. I've made a place for myself here."

"Risking yourself in the arena every night."

"I've found a purpose."

"Fighting for entertainment isn't a purpose, Raiden."

"Remember the first rule of the arena."

Nothing was as it seemed. She frowned. "What—?"

Thorin, Saff, Kace and another gladiator named Lore appeared. All of them were dressed for the arena in leather. Thorin had simple leather straps with a circle of metal over his chest. His axe was on his back, peeking over his shoulders. Kace wore an exquisite leather guard over his right shoulder and arm. Lore wore a black cloak, his tawny hair skimming his broad shoulders. Saff wore leathers like Harper. All the gladiators were hefting their weapons. Saff gave Harper a nod.

"Time to go," Raiden said.

Together, they all moved out of the living area. Galen was waiting for them.

"Do well tonight. Good fighting." His gaze landed on Harper. "You follow what the others tell you, and remember your training. Tonight, Raiden is your fight partner. Thorin will fight with Lore."

She nodded.

"Stay close to me," Raiden ordered.

They moved through a series of tunnels leading up to the main arena. Thorin was trying to lighten the mood with jokes, but Harper was far too nervous to laugh. She felt like she had a rock sitting on her chest.

When they stepped out into the early-evening light, she felt the brush of the breeze on her skin. Then the roar of the crowd hit her.

Two steps ahead of her, Raiden was flanked by Thorin and Kace. Thorin was shaking his enormous axe in the air, while Kace gave a dignified wave.

Raiden did nothing, just stood with his arms relaxed by his side. He didn't pander to the crowds, but they loved him anyway, chanting his name.

Saff slapped Harper on the shoulder. "Good fighting."

"You too."

Harper gripped the hilts of the swords at her hips, turning her attention to the arena proper. Her mouth dropped open. It was completely transformed from what she'd seen the night before. There were rock formations, and even large trees set in place. It was almost like they'd been transported to some forested planet.

"Most of it's holographic." Raiden's voice came from beside her. "They can turn the arena into just about any landscape."

She touched a large rock, feeling the rough surface beneath her palm. "It's incredible."

She saw the others begin to move through their warmup exercises. Harper pulled her short swords from their scabbards. She sliced the blades through the air and glanced around, taking in the cheering crowds, then the House of Galen seats. Galen was standing, arms crossed over his chest, watching them. She swiveled to look at the other side of the arena and her gaze fell on the seats held by the House of Thrax.

Just seeing the aliens—their rough skin with those glowing veins, those horns—made her stomach turn over. Memories hit her like bullets, and she tasted bile in her throat.

She took a deep breath, pushing the feeling of

helplessness away. She was free of them. She wasn't caged in that tiny, featureless cell. And for the last two days, she'd been treated like a person again, and not an animal.

She easily picked out the Thraxian in charge. He looked older, with deep slashes of scars on his face and across his broad chest. He wore an orange sash across his chest.

Then she realized he was looking her way. She held his gaze for a moment, before she turned back to her team. At that moment, the fight siren wailed across the arena, and the crowd went wild.

Harper scanned the rocks and trees, watching for any movement.

Then she saw the first of the beasts lope out of the trees.

She thought it looked like a giant panther. It had dark-black fur, and a huge head, with teeth protruding out of its closed jaws. It moved with a lethal grace, its gaze fixed on them.

Thorin laughed. "Time to play."

Raiden glanced at her for a second, nodded. Then he turned and strode forward with Thorin.

The two of them worked as a team. They barely needed to talk, and it was obvious they'd fought together for a long time. Harper watched the cat leap forward, snapping its powerful jaws. Thorin waved and yelled, snagging its attention, while Raiden came in from the side.

But then Harper saw more huge animals racing over the rocks toward them, with slavering jaws and ferocious, hungry gazes.

Saff stepped up beside Harper. "The Thraxians keep them hungry and tormented. Their imperator is a bastard."

Harper didn't reply because the next second, a *gallu* came lumbering from behind some rocks. It roared, a deafening sound that echoed across the arena.

"Remember the knees," Saff yelled, then charged forward.

Harper followed, swinging her swords around. She kept her muscles relaxed and joined the fight. She went for the *gallu's* knees, and the troll-like creature toppled.

She leaped onto its chest, bringing her swords down to take the killing blow. As the *gallu* slumped beneath her, she looked up and saw another wave of animals heading toward them.

She blocked out the cheers of the crowd and the roars of the beasts, and focused on surviving the fight.

Harper worked with the other gladiators, taking down several creatures. Raiden fought with a cool, efficient style that she found almost mesmerizing. Harper spotted a *raksha* bounding up onto a pile of rocks. The creature was damned graceful, but there was no doubting the raw strength of its powerful body.

She followed it, running up the rocks. Just as she crept up behind it, she saw the cat looking down over the edge. Harper did the same…and spotted Raiden fighting some monstrous creature below. She froze.

The *raksha's* muscles bunched, readying to leap and ambush.

"Oh, no you don't." Harper leaped off the rocks at the same time the creature did.

She hit it midair, jamming her swords in between its ribs. It let out a primal screech and hot blood sprayed across her chest.

Then they were crashing to the ground in a tangle of limbs and claws.

The *raksha* hit the dirt first, and Harper slammed into its body, the air rushing out of her. *Ouch.* Stunned for a second, she dragged in a few breaths. It would have been worse if she'd hit the sand.

Suddenly Raiden was there, pulling her to her feet.

"Thanks."

"Owe you. That *raksha* would have taken me down." He lifted his sword, the inscriptions on it glowing green. "We're not done yet." He pointed his sword.

Coming from between two piles of rocks was a dog-like creature with a ridge of spikes along its back. She wracked her brain for the name of it. A *yeth.* More appeared behind it. A pack of *yeth.*

Together, she and Raiden raced forward. Harper slid on her feet, like a baseball player sliding into base, and cut down two animals.

She turned her head and saw Raiden slash through one *yeth* before he grabbed a second, leaping at him, with his bare hands. With a quick, powerful twist, he snapped the creature's neck and dropped the body.

There were still five more coming, and Harper and Raiden pressed their backs together, swinging their swords in unison.

Harper was covered in blood and gore, but she hadn't felt this alive in such a long time. She turned and saw the rest of the House of Galen gladiators on the other side of the arena, fighting a pack of *rakshas*.

Then she heard gasps from the crowd. She spun, her gaze catching the Thraxian imperator's eyes for a second. He was smiling.

She heard Raiden curse and turned again.

Oh, God. It was like something out of a monster movie. The huge, reptilian creature stood on two legs, towering over them. It had a long, armor-plated tail. Hell, its entre body was armor-plated. It had an elongated jaw, filled with wicked-looking teeth.

"Damn Thraxian scum." Raiden shook his head. "*Gorgo* are banned from the arena. Once they get a taste for blood, they enter a blood-fueled hunting frenzy. It'll slaughter us all and then turn on the crowd."

Jesus. Harper curled her hands around her swords. "Won't someone stop the fight? The authorities?"

Raiden made a scoffing sound. "There are no authorities, Harper. The houses police the fights and this will just make for extra good entertainment. The House of Thrax will get a meaningless warning and pay a token fine."

She blew out a breath. "Okay. So, how do we take it down?"

Raiden shook his head. "See its armor plating? It covers all its weak spots. It's notoriously hard to bring down."

She studied it. It looked like a humanoid killer crocodile. Only, this thing was gigantic.

She and Raiden backed up a few steps, and the creature lumbered forward.

"We aren't supposed to survive this," Raiden said grimly.

Chapter Nine

Raiden was mad.

Damn the Thraxians to the bowels of a black hole. The imperator had to have greased a lot of dirty hands to get the *gorgo* into the arena.

"It breathes fire," he warned Harper.

"Of course it does," she grumbled.

He glanced down at her. There was concern on her face, but no fear. She was fully focused on the creature ahead of them.

"We have a creature that's sort of similar on Earth. Its only weak point is its eyes."

Raiden nodded, spinning his sword. "Same for the *gorgo*. But it's eyes are far above us. They're hard to reach, and it protects them."

"Then we need to bring it down to our level," Harper said. "Can you tangle your net around its legs?"

Raiden considered. "Yes. But I'll have to get close and risk getting set on fire."

She sent him a small smile. "I thought you were a fearless gladiator. Champion of the arena."

"I'm champion because I don't get close enough

to be set alight."

She nodded. "Well, let me take care of that. See the rocks?" She pointed. "I'm going to climb up there and jump across. I'll drop another net on top of its head. While it's busy dealing with that, that's when you need to get in and take out its legs."

Raiden had already seen her jump and knew she could leap higher than any person he'd seen before. Still, he didn't like the idea of her throwing herself out above the *gorgo.*

But the beast was advancing, and they were running out of options. He nodded.

"Keep it busy until I get up there." She set off in a powerful sprint, her arms powering as she ran toward the rocks. She leaped up onto the outcrop like a Neezan gazelle.

Raiden turned back to the approaching *gorgo.* It made a low growling noise, completely ignoring Harper, considering Raiden the biggest threat.

"I fear that'll be a bad mistake," Raiden murmured. He pulled out his net launcher, cradling the device in his palm.

He swung his sword with his other hand. The *gorgo* watched the movement, tensed and cautious. The creature swung one giant claw in Raiden's direction.

Jumping back, Raiden saw Harper reach the top of the rock pile. She was holding her net device, readying to jump.

Come on, my little gladiator. He saw her leap out above the *gorgo.*

Her body was so incredibly graceful yet strong.

She took his breath away. She flew directly over the *gorgo* and dropped her net.

A few inches above the *gorgo's* head, the net deployed. The strong, metal ropes wrapped around the creature's head. It roared, reaching up to bat at the net, which just caught its claws in the wires.

Raiden rushed forward, and flung his net device at the beast's knees.

It let out another ear-splitting roar, and started to fall.

Yes. Smiling, Raiden looked up. His gut cramped. Harper was scrabbling for purchase against the rocks, trying to pull herself up.

Drak. She wasn't going to make it. As he watched, she lost her grip and fell backward.

No. Raiden sprinted forward. He got beneath her and held his arms up. She crashed into his arms and together they fell back and smacked into the dirt, skidding a few feet.

"Okay?"

She nodded. "Thanks."

But another roar suddenly echoed around them, followed by the gasps of the crowd. Raiden and Harper quickly both rolled to their feet.

The *gorgo* was now on its knees, roaring, and fighting the nets holding it down. It blew out a long stream of red-gold fire.

"Damn." Harper looked at Raiden and lifted her swords. "Let's do this."

"Even on its knees, it's still too high for us to reach its eyes," he said.

"Lift me up on your shoulders."

He gripped her, one arm around her waist and the other under her delectable ass and boosted her up. She swung her body, and her legs settled around his head, and for a second, her sweet essence threatened to derail his concentration. That bright, strong feel of her washed over him.

Then she waved her sword. “Go!”

Raiden moved, bringing them closer to the beast. It saw them coming but was still caught in the nets. With a single, strong thrust, Harper jammed one of her swords into the creature’s round eye.

She followed with her second sword, stabbing through a hole in the net, aiming for its other eye. The *gorgo* roared, throwing its head back, and Raiden lunged to the side to avoid the splatter of poisonous green blood.

As the beast’s blood sizzled on the sand, he pulled Harper around and into his arms. He stood, holding her to his chest, as they watched the *gorgo*’s death throes.

A second later, it pitched forward and landed facefirst in the sand. It didn’t move.

“We did it.” Harper looked up, a wide grin on her face. All around them, the crowd went wild. The applause thundered through the arena, louder than Raiden had ever heard before.

“We did.” And then he gave into the craving that had been clawing at him. A need that seemed to keep growing. He tipped her back and pressed his mouth to hers.

She went still, but then her lips opened. He swept his tongue inside, kissing her deeply. She tasted better than the rarest Aurelian ambrosia. He deepened the kiss, hungry for more of her.

"Now the man decides to put on a show for the crowd."

Raiden ignored Thorin's teasing comment and kept kissing Harper. This was for the crowd, he told himself. Just another show for the spectators.

But deep down, he knew that was a lie.

***

Raiden accepted another drink, his gaze glued to Harper on the other side of the corporate box.

After the huge win against the beasts, Galen had bullied them into heading up to the corporate sponsor's area to mingle and celebrate. Raiden took a sip of his ale. More like show them off like prize livestock.

They were all still covered in blood and gore, but that only seemed to make the bigwigs happier. The corporate sponsors—from some inner-galaxy finance world—liked Harper. A man in a shiny suit passed her another ale, and she smiled and took a sip of it.

Was that the kind of man she preferred? One with soft hands and a smooth face?

A body nuzzled into Raiden's side. He glanced down at the woman he couldn't seem to shake. She was dressed in nothing more than a few wisps of fabric, her face heavily painted, and she wasn't being subtle about the fact that she liked hard sex with gladiators. From the moment they'd stepped into the room, she'd attached herself to him.

But Raiden couldn't seem to keep his gaze off Harper.

She'd fought so well in the arena. They'd fought together like they'd been doing it for years. He'd been amazed by her courage and her tenacity.

Moments later, he saw Harper slip out through the doors onto the balcony overlooking the arena. Raiden finally extricated himself from the woman, shoving her over in Thorin's direction, and followed Harper.

She was leaning against the railing, watching the arena below. There was a new match on between two different houses. The House of Thrax had some more new recruits in the arena now. Even from this distance, he could tell they were all petrified and horribly inept.

As he moved up beside her, a starship roared overhead. Harper arched her neck, following the ship as it left Carthago's atmosphere.

"You fought well tonight," he said.

She glanced his way. "Thanks."

"You are now officially a gladiator of the House of Galen."

He saw something flash in her eyes. "I…guess I am." Then she raised a brow. "I thought you were busy." She glanced back toward the door, her face pinched. "Your…company seemed reluctant to let you go."

"There's always some woman willing to spend a night with a gladiator." He leaned against the railing beside her.

Harper made a noise. "So what are you doing out here?"

"The woman I want is out here."

Harper froze and wouldn't look at him.

"You're gutsier than this," he said quietly, caging her against the railing. "You can't just ignore what's between us."

She gave a violent shiver. "I'm attracted to you—"

He laughed. "This is well beyond attraction, Harper, and we both know it." He savored the feel of her. He forgot how small she was because she was such a skilled fighter. He pressed his mouth to her ear, nipping at it. "I don't like it."

She pushed against him. "So stay away."

He knew he should stay away from her. But it was time to admit he couldn't and he really didn't want to.

He was going to take her. Maybe once he'd gorged himself on her, sated his raging need, then this strange obsession would finally fade. "I can't."

She moaned, pressing back against him. "You can have your pick of women." Her voice had turned husky. "I won't just be your flavor of the week."

"I want you." More than he'd ever wanted a woman. He wanted to possess her, own her, and mark her. "And I think you have more than enough flavors for me to handle. Sweet." He kissed her skin. "Sharp. Strong. Hot."

"Raiden…it's been a long time since I've been close to anyone."

"Trust me to take care of you, Harper." He set his teeth against the side of her neck, tasting her salty skin.

She tilted her head to give him better access and he slid a hand down her side, where leather molded her toned curves.

"People can see us here."

"I'll take care of you." He wouldn't let anyone see her. Harper's secret places and her pleasure were his alone.

He flicked open the button on her trousers. She still smelled of sweat and faintly of blood, and it only ratcheted up the primal desire storming through him.

He slid his hand inside her trousers, running his fingers through the damp curls at the juncture of her thighs. He heard her breath hitch. She shifted against him, rubbing against his body.

Raiden groaned, desire rampaging through him. He pushed against her, the hard bulge of his cock rubbing against her ass.

"Are women from Earth different?" he murmured in her ear.

"I have no idea." Her words ended on a gasp and she clamped her hands on the railing.

His finger rubbed through her slick folds. He couldn't wait to strip her bare and explore every inch of her. "Already wet for me, Harper. I want you so badly. I want to sink my cock inside you, or see your lips wrapped around it."

She moaned, looking blindly down at the arena.

Then he felt her go stiff. He frowned. "What is it?"

"It can't be..." She leaned over the railing, staring intently at the fight.

Raiden heard the urgency in her tone. He pulled his hand back and pressed it against her flat belly. He fought to find some control over his throbbing desire.

He glanced back down. The fighters were all shapes and sizes, clearly uncertain about the weapons they were wielding. Most were running around the arena in an attempt to escape any confrontation. He reached over and grabbed some small binocs from a small shelf. They were kept there for the sponsors to use. "Here."

She shot him a grateful glance and snatched the binocs. She held them to her eyes, swiveling until she found what she was looking for.

Then she sucked in a sharp breath. "No."

Raiden grabbed her shoulder. "What? Tell me."

She lowered the binocs, and he could see her face was pale. "The slim fighter on the far right-hand side of the arena. With the pale skin. She's female."

Raiden looked down. He didn't need the binocs to see the small woman. The poor thing was scrambling on her hands and knees, trying to get away from a large opponent sloppily wielding an axe.

"I see her."

Harper turned terrified blue-gray eyes up to him. "That's my friend, Regan. She's from Earth."

Harper pressed her hands to Raiden's chest, her nails digging into his skin. "My friend is in the arena."

Chapter Ten

Harper gripped the railing and tried to leap over it.

Strong arms wrapped around her, pulling her back. "You can't go down there."

She struggled against his hold, watching Regan. Her friend was frightened, stumbling as she tried to get away from the swinging sword of a big alien. Even from this distance, Harper could tell that Regan's clothes were filthy, and that she'd lost weight.

Harper shoved an elbow back against Raiden, but it was like striking rock. As she struggled against his strength, her gaze swung wildly to the House of Thrax's seats. The imperator was watching them. Smiling. The bastard knew that Regan was from Earth, and was taunting her.

She put more energy into her struggles.

Raiden held her tight. "Be smart," he growled into her ear.

Worn out, she sagged in his arms. "How do I get her back?"

She felt Raiden's chest rise as he took a deep breath. "There are ways to help her."

Harper spun to face him. Her face was inches from his tattooed chest. "How?"

A muscle ticked in his jaw, his intense gaze on her face.

He might be a prince with no planet, but he was a powerful man with connections. Harper closed her eyes. She'd always hated asking for help, but Regan needed her.

"Will you help me?" she whispered.

Raiden lifted a hand and ran it over his short hair. "Yes, I'll help you."

Her hands flexed against his chest. Against her will, her palm slid over his hard muscles. "What will it cost me?"

His face darkened, and he stepped away. "I don't need to bribe a woman into my bed. That woman inside will come willingly, and do everything I ask."

Harper lifted her chin, hated the images that splashed in her mind of Raiden and that woman tangled up together. "Raiden—"

He shook his head. "Once we're back at the House of Galen, we'll discuss your friend."

Impatience skidded through her. She turned back, saw Regan sprinting across the arena, trying to escape the gladiators after her. Her friend needed her *now*, not later. Harper gripped the railing so hard, she thought her fingers would crush it to dust.

"She might not have that long."

A hand curled around her shoulder. "Come. I'll talk to Galen. Maybe we can leave this party early."

Raiden was as good as his word. Soon, she found herself being led through a tunnel, squeezed between Raiden and Thorin. Galen was striding in front of them. They passed through the doors of the House of Galen, and she was reluctantly hustled off to shower and change.

Her hair was still wet when she stepped into the gladiators' living area. She was wearing loose-fitting trousers and a tunic top in dark blue.

"Anyone need a drink?" Thorin grabbed a bottle from a shelf of various glass bottles in different shapes and colors.

Kace and Saff were already there, sitting at the long table. Lore and the near-silent Nero were seated on couches. Galen and Raiden stood nearby, talking quietly.

It was then Harper spotted a wall filled with screens and taped images. She frowned at the rolled-up wall hanging. It had concealed all this when she'd been in there today learning her beasts.

She strode over. All the sheets on the wall had pictures of people and information written in some language she couldn't decipher. She saw person after person. Pictures of various fighters down in the arena. Most looked small, far too thin, and not very skilled at fighting.

She turned. "Will someone explain this to me?"

Saff froze with a piece of bread to her mouth. Her gaze sliced across to Kace. Thorin snorted and lifted his feet onto the couch. Raiden's green eyes bored into her.

"What would you like to know?" he asked.

She looked between him and Galen. The imperator had moved over to the bar and mixed an amber-colored drink for himself.

"Back here, you don't look much like slaves and slave master."

Thorin snorted again.

But Harper stared at Raiden. "You aren't a slave."

"No."

"Galen isn't your master."

"No."

He'd warned her. Told her nothing was what it seemed in the arena. She looked back at the images, and spied the slender, winged Pax who'd been sold along with her. She kept looking and also found gentle Ram's image.

"What is this?" She stabbed a finger at the wall.

"They were all people sold to the arena who...shouldn't have been."

Thorin straightened. "What our champion isn't saying is that we help get the weak, the sick, the kidnapped, and struggling out of the arena."

Galen sipped his drink, leaning back against the bar. "We challenge other Houses for them."

"Then G smuggles them out of the arena and off-world," Saff added.

Harper couldn't believe this. She pressed her fingers against her forehead before she forced herself to meet Raiden's gaze. "You're the good guys."

A smile touched Raiden's mouth. "Hardly. I promise you, we aren't good."

"You rescue innocent people."

A slow nod.

She looked at Galen. "You don't enslave people."

Galen lifted his drink. "Correct."

"My friends? Ram and Pax?"

"Safely off-world."

Harper's arms dropped to her sides and she squeezed her eyes closed for a second. Raiden had said he'd found a purpose here but she hadn't understood. "I said some nasty things—"

"Good," Raiden said. "We want everyone outside this room to believe we are what we appear to be."

Thorin snatched up a piece of bright yellow fruit from a bowl filled with them on a low table. He took a large bite. "We want everyone to believe we're big, tough gladiators out for glory. Strong, but not very smart."

Harper pulled in a breath and looked at Raiden. "You can save Regan."

"We can try."

Galen crossed his feet at the ankles, his drink dangling from one hand. "We have an intense…rivalry with the House of Thrax. I suspect their imperator is playing a game, here."

"Word is he's furious he sold you, when you turned out to be a very good fighter," Raiden said.

"Thraxians very much dislike being made fools of," Galen said.

"He knows I'll want Regan," Harper said, dropping into a chair. "He'll make it hard."

"And he saw you and Raiden perform in the ring tonight. Every single person in there saw your…connection. If there is one thing the Thraxian imperator hates more than being fooled, it's Raiden."

Harper ignored the "connection" thing. "Why does he hate you?"

"Because I hate him. I hate every Thraxian." Raiden spun away, his voice gritty. "Because they destroyed my world."

Harper's chest went tight. She stared at the hard lines of his back. The Thraxians had annihilated his entire world. *God.*

"For many years, I've dreamed of annihilating the House of Thrax. Of running my sword through the black-hearted commander who ordered my parents slaughtered and my sister violated."

"Instead," Thorin said. "Raiden makes their life hell. Beats them in the arena, steals their gladiators."

A muscle ticked in Raiden's jaw. "We'll get your friend back, Harper. I promise."

She heard the grim promise in his voice, and she nodded.

But Harper didn't feel a sense of relief. Instead, she felt a sense of dread. Because she realized she and Regan had just landed in the middle of a deadly fight Harper didn't quite understand.

And she didn't think Raiden was going to help simply to free an innocent woman. No, she was worried Raiden had his own dangerous agenda.

***

Raiden strode across the training arena. Ahead, his friends and a few of the new recruits were moving through training exercises. His gaze was drawn to Harper and the way her leather trousers molded over her body.

She was working with a long staff today. She hit at the sand-filled bags that were strung up, took a wrong step, and overbalanced. She cursed under her breath.

He knew she was nervous, waiting for news about her friend. Right now, Galen was off discussing future bouts with the House of Thrax.

Raiden stalked up to her. "Focus."

She turned, her face gleaming with perspiration. "I'm trying."

He leaned close. "Try harder. You enter the arena without complete focus and you'll get hurt. Or worse."

"I'm not a robot." She dropped the staff in the sand and shoved her hands against his chest. "My friend is in danger. I can't just switch off my concern."

He leaned down until his nose brushed hers. "Feeling gets you nothing."

"It gets you friends. I haven't always been the best at it, and I know it's easy to cut yourself off, but that's the coward's way."

Raiden tilted his head, emotions churning through his gut. He lowered his voice. "Are you calling me a coward?"

"Yes."

He felt something electric go through him. "For that, I challenge you."

A wary look crossed her face. "Challenge me?"

He held his hands out by his side. "No weapons. Whoever pins the other wins."

"You can't be serious—"

"The rules of the arena say you cannot refuse a challenge."

Her eyes sparked. "Okay, gladiator. You're on."

They moved apart and circled each other. She moved lightly on her feet, her gaze glued to him, watching and waiting.

He rushed in—a full-frontal attack. She dodged and he felt nothing more than a brush of air against him. He spun.

Just in time to see her foot slam into his belly.

With an *oomf,* he staggered backward. She grinned at him, and it had a mean edge.

They traded more strikes and blows. She was fast, never letting him land anything with his full strength. She got in close, again and again, getting small jabs in under his ribs and onto his lower back.

Each time her body brushed his, it scattered his focus. She was really testing him. Raiden circled around yet again and watched her mimic his moves. She darted in with a quick thrust of her hand. She caught him in the side, and as he moved to block, she shifted and slammed a fist into his gut.

Damn, she was fast. He'd been holding back, but it was time to end this. He reached out for her, but she was waiting. She wrapped her hands around his wrist and dropped her body weight back.

The move pulled him off balance. A small foot

slammed into his knee, and he went sailing over her head.

Raiden slammed into the sand, winded for a second. He bounced up, rolled, and got back to his feet. He saw her grinning at him.

He didn't make a sound. He ran right at her, saw her eyes widen, but she didn't have time to get away. He bent down and scooped her up, tossing her over his shoulder.

"Hey, that wasn't in the rules." She thumped a fist against his back. "Put me down."

As he stalked out of the training arena, he saw the others watching them. The new recruits were all wide-eyed. His friends were all grinning. Raiden ignored them, storming into the tunnel.

Harper was wriggling, trying to get free. He didn't go far before he lowered her and pinned her up against the wall. Then he slammed his mouth down on hers.

She struggled for another second, making an enraged sound against his mouth. Then she caught fire.

Her hands slid over his hair, gripping his skull, and she kissed him back. Their tongues tangled, and Raiden groaned against her mouth, kissed her deeper.

"More." She pulled back, nipping at his lips.

So hungry. He did as she asked. Taking more, pulling the taste of her inside him.

When they finally broke apart, her face was flushed and Raiden felt the fast drum of his heart in his chest. They stared at each other.

"We'll get your friend back," he said.

Harper's lips trembled before she firmed them. That brief show of vulnerability touched something inside him. "Thank you."

"You aren't alone anymore." He slid his hand along her jaw.

Something flickered in her eyes and she pushed her cheek into his hand. "I know."

There was the sound of a clearing throat. They both turned their heads.

Galen was standing beside them, looking highly amused. "I see training is going well."

Harper pushed at Raiden and he stepped back.

"What did the Thraxians say?" she demanded.

Galen's scarred face turned serious. "He said his new acquisition needs time to recover from her first fight."

Harper swallowed. "Is he hurting her?"

"No. She was holding up okay." Now Galen looked at Raiden. "If we want the chance to win Harper's friend, the imperator has demanded two special fights with the House of Galen. If we agree, then he'll let Harper's friend into the arena to be offered up as a prize."

"Two fights." Raiden nodded. That didn't sound too bad.

"One will be tonight. The second one in a few days." Galen crossed his arms. "The imperator demanded that Harper is in the final fight, or all deals are off. If we lose the fight, he wins Harper as the prize."

"No." Raiden shook his head.

Harper spun. “Raiden—”

“I saw the way he watched her. He’s planning something, and we all know Thraxians cannot be trusted.”

Harper grabbed Raiden’s arm. “I have to get Regan.”

Her face was set in stubborn lines. He knew her well enough now to know she wouldn’t back down. That she would do anything, risk anything, to save her friend.

Even her own life.

He both admired and hated that.

Finally, he gave her a single, reluctant nod. What he didn’t tell her was that whatever it took, he would keep Harper safe. Whatever happened, he would be by her side.

Chapter Eleven

The suns were finally starting to set over Kor Magna. Harper swallowed a pained groan. Everything hurt.

She'd put everything she had into her training today. She'd stayed focused on the thought of rescuing Regan, and done her drills over and over again.

Her arms felt like lead, and she was pretty sure even her hair hurt. She couldn't stop worrying about Regan. How was she handling things? How was she holding up?

When she wasn't thinking of her friend, thoughts of Raiden's kiss kept trying to worm in.

Harper lifted her swords, determined to go through another exercise and not think about him, or his kiss, or his hands on her body. She lowered her swords. Her arms were burning too much.

"Earth girl, I think you're done for the day."

Harper looked at Saff. The female gladiator was standing nearby, with her feet shoulder-width apart, and her hands on her hips.

"No. I want to practice a few more—"

"No," Saff said. "I'm not feeling so guilty about snitching on you."

"What?"

Saff smiled. "Angry, overprotective, possessive gladiator incoming."

What? Harper turned, just as Raiden stormed up to her. He grabbed Harper's arm, snatched both of her swords and shoved them at Saff.

"Come on." He pulled Harper across the arena.

She tried to break free. "I have to keep working—"

"You're exhausting yourself." He pulled her into the tunnel. "You'll be no good to anyone, if you're dead on your feet."

"Raiden—"

Suddenly, he jerked to a stop. He grabbed her wrist and touched her explosive cuff.

A second later, it fell free, landing in his palm.

"You've earned this," he said. "You are House of Galen now."

Her mouth opened and she looked up at him, not understanding entirely. But for the first time in her life, she felt a sense of belonging she'd never experienced before.

He grabbed her hand again and pulled her into the living area. Inside, he went straight to a cupboard and pulled out some cloaks. He traded his distinctive red one for one in matte black. Then he fastened a lovely gray cloak around her shoulders.

After that, he tugged her back into the tunnel.

"I'd really appreciate it if you would tell me what's going on," she said. "That would be much better than you dragging me around like I'm a doll."

Green eyes turned her way. “I don’t think you’re a doll.”

When he didn’t add anything else, Harper rolled her eyes. She stayed silent, as he led her into an area she’d never been before. They passed some armed guards, who just waved at Raiden.

And they were outside.

Outside the arena.

She blinked, a hot breeze washing over her. She took in the amazing, hewn walls of the arena behind her, and the maze of two-story, stone buildings ahead of her. The city of Kor Magna stretched out as far as she could see. Most of the nearby two-story buildings looked old, all made of stone, but here and there, she saw communications technology attached to the roofs, and lights glowing.

But not far from the arena, there was a stretch of modern skyscrapers spearing into the sky. There, she saw neon lights blinking, giant billboards flashing, and transports zipping along a wide street. Even from a distance, she could see aliens of all shapes and sizes, humanoid and not, walking the streets.

It made Harper think of the Las Vegas Strip—a jarring spot of bright glitz and glamor.

“The District,” Raiden said, pulling her forward. “It caters to the spectators who come to see the fights.”

“And parts them from their hard earned money.”

He nodded. “Whatever your vice, addiction, or temptation, you can find it in the District.”

There was something in his tone. "You don't like it."

He shrugged. "I don't go there often. I prefer fewer people."

He tugged her away from the bright lights of the District and into the heart of the old city. There were still lots of people here, locals, she guessed. As they walked over the street paved with large rocks, she tried to absorb all the sights and sounds. He took twists and turns, as though he had a specific destination in mind.

"What are we doing out here?" she asked.

"You needed to get out of the arena."

Her heart clenched. He was doing this for her. They traveled down a few more streets and alleys, before Raiden led her to what looked like a giant, circular hole in the ground at the back of an alley.

As they neared it, she frowned. Then she saw a large circular ramp descending downward, hugging the edges of the hole.

They moved downward. "What is this?"

"Carthago is covered in subterranean cave networks and these sinkhole features," he answered. "Because of the soaring temperatures, a lot of people live underground." A faint smile tugged at his lips. "Here in Kor Magna, I think the locals like to hide as much of their city underground as they can, to stop the tourists finding it."

They followed the ramp down, passing a few people toting baskets and bags. Finally, they stepped out into a cavernous underground space.

As her eyes adjusted to the gloom, she gasped. It was filled to the brim with stalls and people. The hubbub of sound echoed off the walls. Light filtered in from the sinkhole and orange lamps attached to the rock walls. She could tell the cavern was mostly natural, the rock the same shade as what the arena was built from.

"Welcome to the Kor Magna Markets," he said.

As he pulled her down a line of stalls, she looked around in wonder. The sights and smells all assailed her. She wasn't surprised to see that most of the stalls were selling things to be used in the arena. One stall was covered in leather gauntlets and armor. Another was selling weapons, and had an excellent display of beautifully crafted daggers. Many were made of metals that Harper couldn't identify. Another stall was selling various poultices and liniments that the seller proclaimed could soothe any aching muscle.

But many were selling strange looking fruits and vegetables, butchered meat, and other household goods.

She noticed a few people eyeing her with curiosity. There was such a range of people of all species here, but she was smaller than...almost everyone. God, she hated standing out.

Harper found herself wandering over to a weapons stall. She ran her finger down the hilt of a beautiful knife. It wasn't just a weapon, it was a work of art. The hilt was carved from a bronze metal and inlaid with blue stones.

She looked up and caught Raiden rolling his eyes.

"What?" she demanded.

"You. You wouldn't care for jewels or baubles for your neck or ears."

She shrugged a shoulder. No, she'd never been a woman to worry about clothes and fancy jewelry.

He tipped her chin up. "I like that. Come on."

They continued on, and soon she smelled the wonderful aromas of things cooking. They moved deeper into the market, and she saw lots of people sitting on low stools and munching on various gourmet delights. Stall owners stood nearby with meat roasting over coals or large pots bubbling. As they passed one stall, she got a whiff of something horrible.

Raiden smiled. "Agama meat. It's a lizard found in the desert here on Carthago. It's a delicacy…if you can stomach the smell."

He stopped at a food stall that had steam wafting off a large barbeque. He purchased two skewers filled with meat, and held up a small round medallion.

"What's that?" she nodded at the medallion.

"A token of the House of Galen. Everything I purchase is charged back to the house."

"So it's like a platinum credit card."

"I do not know what that is." He held out a skewer.

She took it. It was loaded with some sort of delectable-smelling meat. She'd mainly been eating bread, vegetables, and simple meats back at the house. She'd steered clear of anything with strong spices or smells.

"Eat," he ordered.

Since she was hungry, she did. She bit into the meat and the tang of strange spices broke out across her taste buds. She moaned. "What is this?"

"The meat of the corra serpent that lives in the desert."

She paused. "A serpent. Ah, maybe it's better you don't tell me." She took another bite. As she licked her fingers, she looked up and saw Raiden was staring at her.

"What?"

"You eat like you do everything else. With every bit of your energy and enthusiasm."

His words and his gaze made her heart knock into her ribs. "You going to eat yours?"

He nodded and bit into the meat.

Harper waited while he finished. After he'd disposed of the skewers, he held up a cloth and dabbed at her mouth. He wiped once, twice, and then it was his callused thumb rubbing across her lips.

Her breath hitched. "This…attraction isn't going away, is it?"

"No," he answered.

"Neither of us want or need this."

"Correct."

She resisted the urge to kick him. Everything was true, but he didn't have to sound so matter-of-fact about it. "This would just be a big problem for us—"

He cupped her cheeks. "For the moment, let's not worry about problems. You're here to enjoy yourself."

Abruptly, he grabbed her hand. Holding her tight, he pulled her back into the crowded market again. They moved off into some side tunnels. She could see that not all were natural and some had been carved out to make more room.

Here and there, sellers were calling out, hawking their wares. Harper felt herself relaxing. Her capture, her captivity, her time in the arena, worry for Regan, it all had her walking the very fine edge of stress and anxiety.

In this moment, she could just relax for a few minutes. Pretend she was nothing more than a tourist, and not worry about anything.

He pulled her down through a stone archway. There were more stalls packed into this space, and he stopped at one particular one. It appeared to sell leather harnesses and scabbards. As he haggled with the stall owner, whom he seemed to know, she wandered over to look at the leather harnesses. They looked identical to the ones Raiden wore in the arena.

Then Raiden turned and came to her side. He held out a small, round medallion.

Harper took it, turning it over. It had a fastening on the back. She turned it to the front again, studying the beaten-metal surface and the decoration carved into it.

It was the twin to the one he wore on his harness.

"It's for you," he said.

"Thank you." God, when was the last time someone had given her a gift? "It's beautiful."

"It's a design from my planet. It reminds me of you, a beautiful design but made of solid steel."

She bit down on her lip, touched. Something from his planet. The planet that had been destroyed. "What was your world called?"

Raiden lifted his head, looking out across the market. "Aurelia."

A beautiful name.

"We were at war with a neighboring planet. A feud that had gone on for generations. When I was sixteen, that planet hired a team of advanced, ruthless mercenary fighters. They invaded under the cover of darkness and decimated my planet."

She gasped. "Mercenaries."

Hard green eyes met hers. "The Thraxians. They killed my mother, my father. My younger sister was raped before my eyes."

God. Harper had no words. Instead, she leaned into him. She knew he'd been a prince, so it made sense that the royal family had been targeted.

"The mercenaries planted powerful bombs in the fault lines of my planet. After they were set off, they started a chain reaction. Aurelia was ripped apart."

She closed her eyes. "How did you get away?"

"I tried to fight back, but there were too many of them, and I was young. I was injured. My bodyguard got me off the planet."

Understanding bloomed. "Galen."

Raiden gave a single nod. “He’s only a few years older than me. He was raised to be my royal bodyguard from birth.”

“So your world is gone.” She pressed a hand to his back, felt the muscles beneath her fingers flex. “And so is mine. It’s too far away for me to ever get back.”

They stared at each other. How could she feel so much so quickly for this tough man?

Without another word, Raiden grabbed her hand. Once again, they moved through the labyrinth of tunnels. She saw the way the people acted when they recognized him. She saw awe, excitement, trepidation and fear. He was a larger-than-life god to them.

But Harper was starting to see that beneath the tough gladiator was just a man.

As they moved on, she saw some tunnels leading into darker, seedier looking areas. Groups of men lounged against walls smoking. She realized that there were darker, scarier things hidden down here as well.

But soon they moved back into a well-lit area with a smooth stone floor. Raiden stopped in front of a wooden door banded by beaten metal.

He pulled out a key and opened the door. After he locked it behind them, they went down a spiral stone staircase until they came out into a large room.

Harper gasped. A large pool filled the space. A mosaic tile floor covered the bottom of the water that sparkled blue, lit by hidden lights. By the side of the pool was a seating area of large cushions. It was ringed by potted plants and a pretty vine that covered the stone wall.

"You said you liked to swim," he said.

"It's beautiful," she said.

He moved toward the pool's edge. "I did too, as a boy on Aurelia. It had many beautiful lakes."

And he must have missed it terribly when he came here. She touched the thick, wild vine growing on the wall. It was covered in tiny, delicate flowers that gave off a beautiful perfume.

She breathed deep. "That scent is delicious." She sucked it in.

"It's called *phena*. Some say it's an aphrodisiac."

Oh? Harper felt an insidious curl of heat in her belly. "What is this place?"

"It is owned by the House of Galen."

But it was his. She knew it. She bit her lip. Maybe this was his private little pleasure pool. "Do you bring all your arena admirers here?" She felt acid burning in her belly.

He looked down at her, pulling her closer. "I've never brought anyone here. These plants—" he fingered the dark, waxy, red leaves of a slender potted tree. "They are nocturnal plants originally from Aurelia. I've spent years tracking down the seeds."

Raiden pulled her over to where the large cushions sat. She sank down on one the same color as the cloak he wore in the arena.

"I admire your spirit, Harper." He stayed standing, his cloak framing his powerful body.

"And your essence."

"My essence?"

"Aurelians can feel a person's personality."

Wow. "That's…amazing."

"It's how I tracked you the night you escaped. Your essence is strong and bright. I feel your sadness, but you don't drown in it. You let it inspire you."

"Like you do."

He remained silent.

"You do, Raiden." She tucked her legs beneath her. "You're helping others. You're thriving in the arena."

He looked away. "I had nothing left. Now I do as I please."

"Bullshit."

He tilted his head. "My lingual translator does not know that word."

"It's an expression we use on Earth. Let's just say, I don't think you're telling me the truth."

His face tightened. "I do not care for others. I care only for myself."

"Bullshit," she said again. "Galen, Thorin, Saff, and the others. You have a lot of people you care about."

"Because they are useful to me." He turned away, staring at the water.

Harper got to her feet. "Why do you pretend you don't care—?"

Raiden spun quickly, grabbing her arms. "Because it hurts too much when you lose them. They slaughtered my parents, my sister, the entire population of my planet. People who depended on me and my family to protect them." As suddenly as he grabbed her, he let her go and turned away.

She touched his back. "I'm sorry, Raiden." All this pain. Had he been carrying it around all these years? How did he bear it?

"I failed them," he said. "I can still see Naida's face as they hurt her. Begging me to help her."

"I lost my sister, too." That pain she could truly understand.

He stared at her. "I'm sorry."

"I know what it feels like, Raiden."

He let out a shuddering breath. "You keep pushing and digging under my skin. I don't like it."

His sharp words made her take a step away. "Fine. So stay away from me."

He whipped his head around to stare at her. His gaze was blazing. "I can't seem to."

Harper felt a crazy mix of emotion. "I'm going to swim." She looked around. "Are there swimsuits?"

"No. I always come alone."

She wasn't letting that stop her. Harper turned her back on him and pulled her clothes off. She could feel his gaze on her and dammit, she liked it. Far too much.

She dived cleanly into the water.

Oh, God. It felt so good. She kicked and found her rhythm, swimming some laps. She saw Raiden cut into the water, swimming beside her.

His big powerful body was naked.

A shiver ran through her. Finally, she stopped swimming and floated at the surface. She watched

Raiden's strong arms slice through the water, before he stopped near her.

"Thank you for bringing me here," she said quietly.

He kept staring at her and the clear water did nothing to block her view of his naked body. Or the long, thick cock rising up against his belly.

He swept her into his arms, and pressed a punishing kiss to her lips.

Whenever he touched her, she went up in flames. All her control evaporated like smoke. All she wanted to do was touch every inch of him, taste every part of him, know him.

"Raiden—"

"Yes." One harsh word.

Their hands were all over each other. She circled his heavy cock, stroking it. *Take. Lose yourself in him. Oblivion, just for a little while.*

But it would be temporary and empty. She ripped her mouth from his. "Let me go."

He made a scary sound. "You want this. You want me."

She shook her head. "Maybe, but you don't want to take the risk of caring. Nor do I."

"Bullshit," he said, his pronunciation perfect. His hands cupped her breasts.

She grabbed his wrists. "I need more than just lust, Raiden. I want to lose myself in you, but I can't do it knowing I'd be just another warm body in your bed." Hell, she was so confused. She didn't want to get close, but she wanted him more than she wanted to breathe. But she tried one more time. "We need to stop."

"I see you, Harper Adams. I want *you*."

Dammit. She went back up on her toes to kiss him. He swung her into his arms like she weighed nothing. He strode out of the pool and the next second, he lowered her down onto the pillows. God, she wanted his hands on her skin.

"If you do not want this, Harper, you must tell me." He pressed a kiss between her breasts, one big hand coming up to cup one globe. "Say no, and, I'll stop touching you. I'll never touch you again."

They stared at each other, and a part of Harper's brain told her to say that little word.

She opened her legs, letting his big body fall into hers. She saw wild satisfaction cross his face.

He leaned down and lavished her breasts with attention. She arched into him. His tongue moved over her skin and he tugged her nipple into his mouth, letting her feel the edge of his teeth. She grabbed his head. "Yes."

He moved lower, scraping his scruff over her belly. Lower.

Then he was pushing her legs apart. Harper found herself naked against the soft pillows, her big, rough galactic gladiator poised above her.

"I wanted to taste you from the first moment I saw you," he growled.

His hand slid up her thigh and then dipped into her folds. Harper made a sound, lifting her hips to his touch.

"So wet for me. It appears human women of Earth are not so different." He stroked her, sliding a thick finger inside her.

She moaned. God, that was just his finger.

"You are very tight." His voice deepened, took on an edge. "We'll have to work hard to get me inside you."

Yes. She wanted him stretching her. He lifted his hand, his fingers glittering with her juices. He brought them to his mouth, sucking them clean.

Harper's belly contracted. So dirty and so sexy.

His mouth hovered over her and she felt his warm breath on her. "Raiden—"

He moved and she felt the scratch of his stubble on her thigh. "I'm going to taste you now." Then he licked her.

She jerked. God, that warm, rough tongue... When his mouth closed over her, she cried out. Her hands slid down to his head, pushing him closer. His tongue stabbed inside her. It felt so good. So damn good.

"Tell me what you like," he growled against her skin. "What pleases you most?"

She nudged him until his tongue flicked at her clit. She bucked upward with a cry.

Raiden sat back, an intense, curious gaze on his face. He probed her clit with his finger. "Well, maybe you are a little different." He circled it, watching her reaction.

Harper felt the blood pumping through her system, every cell in her body throbbing. She strained up, needing, wanting more.

"What is this?" he asked.

"My..." God, she couldn't believe they were

having this conversation. “My clitoris, my clit. It’s...”

He circled it again and she jerked her hips up. “The center of your pleasure.”

“Yes. Raiden, please.”

He leaned over her. “Tell me. What do you want, Harper?”

“Lick me. Suck me.”

He moved back to her clit, sucking her.

It was too much and it wasn’t enough. As her release crashed into her, she wrapped her legs around his head, and screamed his name.

Chapter Twelve

Raiden had never had a woman come alive under his touch like Harper. She was so responsive, so hungry, so greedy.

She was still making husky sounds, small shivers going through her body. He pressed a kiss to her inner thigh, then he stood.

She looked up at him through heavy eyelids. Her rapid breathing was making her full breasts heave and Raiden took in every inch of her. He felt like he was going to explode.

"I want you to touch me," he demanded.

"Oh?"

"I want your mouth on my cock. Now."

She got up on her knees. "I don't like bossy men."

"Harper, suck my cock."

She moved closer, her hands pressing to his thighs. Her short nails dug into his skin. "You are too used to getting your own way."

Pushing the edge, he made a growling sound.

Suddenly, she moved, leaping up and taking him down. He landed on the soft pillows with Harper straddling him.

"Luckily, I seem to like it," she murmured. "Mostly." She scooted back until his cock was in her hands. Her eyes widened. "Oh."

Raiden paused, watching her as she looked at him. "Am I…different from the men of Earth?"

"Ah, just a little larger." She wrapped her fingers around his thick cock and pumped.

She dragged her tongue across the head of him. Raiden swallowed a groan and let her lick at him. Then she opened her mouth and took him in.

She moved slowly at first, adjusting to his size.

"Relax," he murmured.

But it didn't take her long to find her rhythm, bobbing her head and sucking him deep. He felt his cock hit the back of her throat, but she swallowed, moaning on him.

Damn. He tangled his hand in her hair, pushing her down deeper so she took more of him. She was driving him crazy and he was losing control. He never lost control.

He felt his body tensing, his hips thrusting up against her mouth, but he couldn't quite let go.

She pulled off him. "I've got you, Raiden. I'm here." Her gaze met his, and then, keeping eye contact, she lowered her mouth down on him, sucking him between her lips.

Raiden couldn't hold back any longer. He came with a roar. As he spilled himself inside her mouth, he felt Harper's hands stroking him, her mouth sucking every drop.

He yanked her up into his arms, holding her

tight. Her arms moved around him. Raiden buried his face in her hair and for the first time in a very long time, just let himself enjoy the feel of a woman.

She nuzzled into him, her skin still damp. But he wasn't done with her yet. Far from it.

He rolled her under him again, covering her with his body.

Her eyes went wide. "You're ready…again?"

"Aurelian men come two or three times in quick succession."

Her mouth opened in an O. Her beautiful breasts, topped with pink nipples captured his attention. He leaned down, sucking on them. She writhed beneath him.

He slid his hand down her body and her hips rolled against him. Finally, he was sliding a finger inside her. Damn, she was tight, but she was also wet, making the entry smooth for him. His cock was going to feel so good sliding inside her. He pumped her harder, loving her responsive moves and cries.

"I want to bury myself deep inside you, Harper."

"Fuck me, Raiden. Please."

"Where do you want my cock?"

"Inside me." Her head dropped back.

Raiden reared up, holding her in his lap. "Let me see your eyes, Harper."

Blue-gray eyes came back to him. He lifted her with one hand while his other circled his throbbing cock. He lowered her down, the head rubbing through her damp folds.

As he entered her, she moaned. He'd never heard a more beautiful sound. He pumped his hips up, slowly working inside her. She was so damned tight.

"You're too big," she whispered.

"No, I'll fill you up just right." He pumped inside her again, finally buried all the way inside her.

He filled his hands with the sweet curves of her ass and started to move. She cried out, and the sound of their bodies slapping together filled the room.

"Again. More."

Raiden couldn't handle any more. He thrust hard, hearing her cry as he went deep, then he pushed her back on the pillows and started to hammer inside her. "I could live here. Right here. My cock will never get enough of you."

"Yes." She arched up, taking everything he gave her. Then her body clamped down on his, and she screamed his name.

He dragged his cock out of her and rammed home one last time. His body jerked, and he threw his head back, as his orgasm slammed into him and he came deep inside her body.

He dropped his forehead to hers, trying to pull air into his burning lungs. He couldn't seem to form any words, so he just stayed there, buried inside her, and pressed his face against her neck.

"Don't let me go," she murmured against his skin.

"I won't." And Raiden knew that wasn't a lie. He wasn't done with her and a part of him wondered if he ever would be.

***

Harper took her time cleaning the weapons. She wiped the oiled cloth along the blade of each sword. She'd already completed one wall of weapons in the weapons room. She only had a few more to take care of.

The room was packed with weapons from all around the galaxy. The walls were covered in swords, daggers, and staffs. Racks filled the space and held axes, nets, and various other weapons she didn't recognize.

But all her attention wasn't on the blades. No, her chaotic thoughts all starred one sexy, tattooed gladiator, and what they'd done to each other yesterday evening. She was more than a little sore between her legs.

Harper blew out a breath and smiled to herself. She'd had several lovers in her lifetime, but nothing could quite equal what she'd shared with Raiden in that subterranean pool.

God, he'd been insatiable. He'd taken her again on the edge of the pool and he'd given her the longest, strongest orgasms she'd ever experienced. Oh, it was so easy to imagine that big cock of his sliding inside her, filling her up.

They'd stayed by the pool, sleeping on the pillows in a tangle of limbs. They'd snuck back into the House of Galen at sunrise.

The sound of quiet footsteps made her shake her

head. She'd better focus on what she was doing or she might just slice a finger off with one of these swords.

"Mistress."

Harper's head jerked up. She saw a young woman standing nearby in a simple white dress—she'd learned this was the standard garb household servants wore. Her head was bowed and she didn't make eye contact, but Harper didn't think she'd seen her before. "Ah, can I help you?"

"For you." The woman moved forward and held out a small piece of paper.

As Harper took it, the woman hurried away, disappearing out of the room and down the corridor. Harper glanced at the paper. It wasn't like paper on Earth. It was tougher, more fibrous, and made her think of old-fashioned papyrus.

She flicked it open. There were words scrawled on it...in English?

Harper. I need to see you. It's important. The guards will let you through at midday today. Come alone.

Harper's muscles locked. The writing was shaky, but she'd seen Regan's scrawl in her notebooks back on the space station. It was definitely her friend's handwriting. Harper stroked a finger across the writing.

Quickly, she folded the paper and slipped it into the pocket of her leathers. She tapped her foot on the ground. She should tell Raiden about this. She shook her head. He'd order her not to go. Hell, he'd probably lock her up. She knew it was insanely risky to sneak into the House of Thrax...

Harper assessed the risks. They were high. But she was trained, she wasn't defenseless this time. She *had* to see Regan and getting caught was worth the risk.

Harper kept herself busy for the next few hours, waiting impatiently for the suns to reach their zenith. She timed her escape when the others were heading into the dining room to eat their midday meal. As soon as she saw Raiden and the others enter the large dining area, she grabbed a basket of damaged gauntlets and ducked out into the tunnels.

As she approached the main doors of the House of Galen, she took a deep breath. Stay calm. Act like you belong.

The guards both eyed her. "What are you doing here?"

She lifted the basket. "Need to drop these guards and armor pieces off for repair."

The guards frowned at each other. "We have no authorization of this."

She shrugged. "No skin off my nose." When they both just stared at her, she shook her head. "I mean, it doesn't bother me." She held the basket out. "You guys can get them where they need to go. I know Raiden won't be happy if his favorite harness isn't ready for the fight tonight."

Both guards straightened.

"Fine," the taller one said. "Go. Take it and get back here."

She nodded and hurried out into the main

tunnel. She walked through the tunnel network, heading toward the House of Thrax. She'd studied a map of the arena and its tunnels on the wall in the gladiators' living area. She just prayed she didn't get lost.

How had Regan convinced the guards to look the other way? God, Harper just hoped her friend was okay. She needed to talk to Regan, see for herself she was unharmed. She had to tell Regan to hold on, that she was going to get her out.

A memory hit. *I'm going to help you, Brianna. Just reach out and let me help you.* Harper's steps faltered. She hadn't been able to save her sister, but this time, she wasn't going to fail.

Harper reached the corridor leading to the House of Thrax and stowed her basket in an alcove. She waited in the shadows around the corner, staring at the double doors made of beaten copper-colored metal. They had a logo with a set of horns on it—the symbol of the Thraxians. Two alien guards stood flanking the doorway.

It had to be midday. So what did she do now? Ask the guards to just let her in?

The next minute, the doors to the House of Thrax opened, and she saw the young woman who delivered the message arrive, holding a tray of drinks. The woman laughed quietly with the guards, passing the drinks to them. They moved to the side of the open door.

Harper took the opportunity.

She forced herself not to rush, and kept her steps quiet. She reached the door, and while the men were tipping back their goblets, she slipped inside.

Unlike the House of Galen, inside the House of Thrax was very dark. Through the shadows, she could see the bars of the cells lining both walls. Somewhere ahead, she heard someone moaning in pain. She swallowed. *God.*

Harper quietly crept along the cells, searching inside for any sign of Regan. She saw many different species sitting on the dirt-packed floors, slumped over, heads buried in their hands or curled up in a fetal-type position. One man looked up and bared his sharp teeth at her.

She moved on, and then caught a flash of pale skin in the darkness. A woman was curled up on the floor, matted hair hiding her face. She looked about Regan's size.

"Regan," Harper whispered.

The woman lifted her head.

Harper gasped, shock reverberating through her. It was Rory Fraser, Regan's cousin.

Rory pushed to her feet, her red curls tangled around her face. "Fuck me, Harper. Is it really you?"

Harper reached through the bars and gripped Rory's hand. "Sure is."

A shudder wracked the woman's fit body. Her face was covered in dirt and bruises. One of her eyes was swollen shut.

Harper moved to test the cell door. It was locked tight.

There was movement from the cell beyond Rory's.

"Harper?" A harsh whisper. "Oh, my God, Harper."

Regan stood with her arms wrapped around her curvy body. Harper's heart leaped, her throat closing. They were alive.

"It is so good to see you," Harper said.

"You shouldn't be here," Regan said quickly.

"I'm going to get you out of here." Harper searched the cells. "Have you see Madeline? She was taken with me?"

Both women shook their heads.

"You shouldn't have come." Regan's eyes met Harper's and her face blanched. Her gaze moved over Harper's shoulders, her mouth opening—

A hard blow slammed between Harper's shoulder blades. As she slammed into the bars, she slid down and turned. A kick caught her in the ribs, pain flaring. She looked up and saw Thraxian guards rushing out of the shadows, their veins glowing orange.

She heard Rory cursing and Regan shouting.

A trap. *Dammit to hell.* She'd walked right into it with her eyes wide open.

Harper reached for her swords, and mentally she cursed herself. She wasn't wearing them.

She kicked out with her foot and toppled the closest guard. When the next one rushed at her, she ducked under his sword, and jammed a fist into his armpit. When he grunted, she swung around and thrust the edge of her hand against his lower back. He went down to his knees, dropping his sword.

Harper scooped the sword up and twirled. The blade of her sword slammed against the one the next Thraxian held. Metal clanged on metal as she fought. But more were coming.

Too many more.

Two of them rushed her at once. She blocked one sword, but the second guard's sword sliced into her shoulder.

She felt the hot burn and then the rush of warm blood. Her white shirt bloomed red.

"Harper!"

She heard Regan's shout, but ignored it. She kept swinging. There was no way she could rescue the women right now. She cast a frustrated look at the cells. As she kept bleeding, dizziness rocked her. She wasn't even sure if she could make it out of here alive.

Another guard came in close. He was carrying a baton and slammed it down hard on her sword arm. With a cry, her sword clattered to the ground.

All around, the prisoners were shouting and banging against the bars of their cells. The din was deafening.

More dizziness made her stomach turn over and she staggered. She wasn't going to make it.

She thought of Raiden. Just his face. She raised her good arm. She was going to take down as many Thraxians as she could.

Taking a step back, she ran into a hard body. No.

But arms wrapped around her and Thorin's massive form rushed past her. As he engaged the remaining guards, Harper was turned around so fast, her head spun.

She looked up into Raiden's frightening enraged face.

He didn't say anything, just looked at her blood-soaked shirt, and then scooped her up into his arms.

"Raiden—"

"Quiet."

The harsh word made her wince.

Behind them, Thorin had taken down the final few guards. "Let's go." He swung his axe up on his shoulder. "We'll have more company soon, and it's best we aren't caught in here."

As Raiden carried her away, she tried to see Regan and Rory, but they were lost in the shadows. They exited the House of Thrax, and in the main corridor, she saw the two guards slumped against the wall, unconscious.

Raiden and Thorin quickly moved through the tunnels, heading back toward the House of Galen.

"I got a message from Regan," she said quickly. "I had to come. It said to come alone."

"You talk of trust, but it is all lies."

Raiden's words were like a well-aimed sword slashing at her heart. "I'm sorry—"

"I said be quiet."

They stepped back into the House of Galen, and Raiden slammed into the living area. He strode through another doorway into a smaller room. It had smooth, plastered walls and a huge bed covered in furs.

His bedroom. He dumped her on the bed and went back to the door. "Thorin, bring me the healing kit."

Then Raiden strode back to her and grabbed the neckline of her shirt. With one pull, he tore it, barely missing the nasty cut from the guard's sword. Raiden's eyes narrowed, and he looked even more dangerous. Anger pulsed off him in waves.

Thorin appeared and dumped a leather bag on the bed, before shooting Harper a sympathetic look and leaving the room.

Raiden took a moment to sort through the bag and pulled out a clean wad of fabric and a tube. He squirted a blue substance on the fabric and wiped away the blood on her skin. His gentle touch was at odds with the scary look on his face.

He squirted more gel on the wound, rubbing it in with the lightest touch.

"It will be healed within a few hours," he said.

"I had to see her, Raiden. And there is another woman from my space station there."

He stayed silent.

"They're all I have left," she whispered.

He stared at her. "You could have had more here, if you'd wanted them."

He spoke in the past tense. She felt another burn of heat under her heart, but she also felt anger. "Oh? You've made it clear it's better to stay alone. To not care."

Raiden stood in one fluid move of his powerful

body. A muscle ticked in his jaw. "I will kill the Thraxian imperator for luring you there."

Harper closed her eyes. *God.* Even while he was insanely angry at her, he was still trying to protect her. "It's always about vengeance with you, isn't it?"

"I have a fight to prepare for." He spun on his heel and stormed out.

Harper sagged back against the bed and pulled her shirt around herself. She could smell him on the covers. Thorin's big presence filled the doorway.

"Haven't seen him that angry in a long time."

"Thanks, Thorin. You're making me feel much better."

"Not here to make you feel better, little gladiator. You screwed up."

She turned her head to face him. "You want to kick me a little? Maybe stab me with a sword again?"

His gaze ran over her, the corner of his mouth tilting up. "Nope. Don't think you can feel much worse than you do right now." He turned to leave as well, but paused. "You may not know Raiden well enough yet, but his bark is usually worse than his bite."

She snorted, wrapping her arms around herself. His bark was bad enough.

"He was a ball of rage when I first met him, but over the years, he learned to lock it down. When he gets really angry..." Thorin's gaze met hers "...it's because he really cares, even if he won't admit it."

With that excellent parting shot, Thorin left her alone.

Chapter Thirteen

With single-minded focus, Raiden kept slamming his hands into the gel-filled punching bags at the edge of the training arena.

Sweat was pouring off him. He'd been at it for a few hours.

He heard heavy footsteps and recognized them as Thorin's. Since he still wasn't in the mood for talking, Raiden didn't bother turning around.

"So, you destroyed the sparring dummy and the sword target. Now you're going to hit that bag until it bursts."

"Yes."

Thorin snorted. "I never thought I would see the day when the mighty Raiden fell for a woman."

Raiden slammed his fist into the bag harder than before, sending the bag shaking. "I don't know what you're talking about."

"Why do you deny what you feel for her?"

Raiden stayed quiet, flexing his torn knuckles. He kept seeing Harper in the middle of the House of Thrax, blood soaking her shirt. He looked down at his own blood-stained hands and knew some of it was hers.

"I think I know," Thorin said.

Raiden turned, pressing his hands to his hips. “Don’t you have anything better to do?”

“No. Watching you being an ass is too entertaining.”

Raiden turned back to his bag and started punching it again.

“You like her,” Thorin continued. “You care about her. You’re pissed she went off on her own and got herself hurt. That’s understandable.”

“Caring for someone makes you weak.”

“I know you care, Raiden. Not just for Harper. And you’re one of the strongest men I know. You pulled me out of the darkest place I’ve ever known, and put me back together.”

Raiden’s hands stopped. He and Thorin never spoke of those dark days when the man had first come to the arena. “You would have saved yourself.”

“No, I wouldn’t have. Besides, something makes me think that a woman like Harper…she’d make you stronger.”

Raiden heaved in a breath, thinking of Harper using her swords, focusing on winning the fight. Of Harper’s small cries as she came under his mouth.

Thorin’s voice lowered. “I’d really like to know what you are thinking right now.”

When Raiden spun around, Thorin shot Raiden a wily grin.

“You can’t protect everyone, Raiden. She’ll accept you standing by her side, but she’ll never let you lock her away. I know you lost everybody you loved, but—”

"Save it, Thorin. I don't want to hear it."

His friend sighed. "Yeah, I can see that. By the gods, you have a hard head."

Raiden heard a horn blare. He abandoned the bag and strode over to the weapons racks. He pulled his harness on, his cloak falling into place behind him. For a second, he touched the medallion on his chest. "I have a fight."

"Yeah." Thorin shook his head. "My pity to the poor opponents you take your anger out on tonight."

***

Harper tried to control her nerves. She stood in the House of Galen seats, one cold hand on the railing, watching Raiden and the others fighting below.

It was a simple fight. There were no chariots, beasts, or anything fancy. Just good, old-fashioned fighting.

But she was still nervous. She scanned around and spotted the Thraxian imperator moving into the House of Thrax box. The big alien sat in his seat, directly across the arena from Harper.

And then Harper spotted Regan.

Rage pulsed through her. Her friend was chained by her neck and shoved to sit at the imperator's feet. Harper breathed through her nose, trying to control the need to rush over there and beat the imperator in the face.

"Keep it together."

The deep voice was barely more than a rumble.

Harper didn't even spare a glance for the big, silent gladiator who was like a mountain standing beside her.

"Nero, you've never spoken to me before. Why start now?"

"Raiden asked me to watch you."

Harper wasn't sure if that made her happy or angry. Raiden. He hadn't spoken to her since he'd rescued her.

He'd shut her out. Like they'd never touched each other.

Don't think of him. She looked over at Regan. *Hold on, Regan. Two fights and you'll be safe.*

Harper forced herself to look back at the arena. Raiden was mowing through his opponents, leaving them writhing in the sand.

Yes, he was on a tear tonight. She almost felt sorry for the House of Thrax gladiators. She watched two more of them fall.

They weren't offering Raiden much challenge. She frowned. The fight was easy. Too easy.

And then she heard the crowd gasp.

Harper jerked to her feet, her heart hammering in her chest. She turned and saw that Raiden was staggering backward.

A spear had pierced his chest.

No. As she watched, he gripped the long pole and yanked, pulling it out of his flesh.

She let out a shaky breath. Yes, he was big and strong, but blood was pouring down his chest. How was he still even on his feet?

"He's strong, Harper," Nero said.

She glanced at the gladiator, but saw he looked concerned. Farther down the row, Galen was also on his feet.

"Damn Thraxian bastards," Galen muttered. "It was a sneak attack, not out in the open and honorable."

Harper was pretty sure the Thraxians didn't give a shit about honor. "How's he still on his feet?"

"Aurelians are bred tough," Galen answered, his single pale eye glittering.

She saw Thorin, Kace and the others close in around Raiden. Raiden was talking to Thorin, so that was good.

She looked back at the Thraxian gladiators. There was still a large group of them left standing. Eight…no nine.

But the crowd gasped again. She spun and watched, horrified, as Raiden collapsed onto the sand.

Harper curled her hands around the railing, willing him to get up. The Thraxian fighters rushed forward, trying to get to him.

The House of Galen gladiators met them, weapons swinging.

She sensed Galen move. He was closer to the railing now, his scarred face blank of emotion.

"What's wrong?" she demanded.

"Poison."

A cold wind blew through her. The others had warned her that the House of Thrax were known for their debilitating poisons.

She watched as the others fought the final

fighters, but every minute that ticked by felt like an eternity. Raiden needed medical help.

Then she saw a huge Thraxian get past Galen's gladiators. He headed straight for Raiden's still form.

No. Harper reached over and yanked Galen's sword from the scabbard at his waist.

As she whirled, she heard him curse. But Harper gripped the railing, and with one lithe move, she pushed herself over.

"Harper!" Galen's hands brushed her.

She landed in the arena in a crouch, feeling sand sink into her shoes. Then she pushed up and raced across the arena.

The Thraxian was almost at Raiden's side, lifting his axe with a smile.

He didn't see her coming. She came in from the side, slamming her sword against his hand where it held his axe. He screamed, his weapon hitting the sand.

But he wasn't down. He swung out his other huge fist and Harper leaped backward to avoid him. She had no armor, just her simple clothes. She couldn't let him strike her. She didn't let her panic overcome her. She had to protect Raiden.

She swung her sword again, but he dodged. She took the risk, getting in close, and sliced a nasty cut across his belly.

He staggered backward. Another gladiator appeared and her weapon met his. She let her rage fuel her and she forced him back, finally taking him down with a slice across his thigh. Blood spilled onto the sand.

Footsteps behind her. She spun, lifting her sword.

"Whoa." Saff raised a hand. "Easy, Harper. Fight's over. And the House of Thrax will have to answer for that dirty little poison trick."

Harper blinked, trying to calm herself. She saw all the Thraxian gladiators were down and the crowd was cheering. Chanting Raiden's name.

She raced across to Raiden, falling to her knees beside him. His muscles were tensed, straining. Paralyzed, she realized. But his eyes were open, his gaze raw and intense. He looked like he was in agony.

"You'll be okay." She brushed a hand over his forehead. "Just hold on."

"We need to get him out of here," Thorin shouted.

Kace and Thorin moved, one to Raiden's feet and the other to his head. They lifted his prone body between them. Saff, Lore, and Harper provided cover as they carried him out of the arena.

Galen met them in the tunnels. "Hurry. I have our healers waiting." He looked at Harper and held out a hand. "My sword."

She handed it over and hurried to stay by Raiden's side. He'd be okay. He was Raiden. Champion of the Kor Magna Arena.

They reached the House of Galen. Galen held the door open. "Get him into Medical."

Harper had never been in Medical. The lights were bright, and the place looked far more high-tech than anything else she'd seen here. Three large, rectangular tanks, filled with a blue fluid, sat against the back wall.

Two tall Hermia healers moved over, their beige robes whispering quietly around their slender bodies. "Place him in the central tank, please." The lead healer's voice was soft, almost melodious.

Harper moved back. She saw Raiden was breathing shallowly, perspiration dripping off his face. His gaze met hers and she felt seared by it.

They stripped Raiden of his clothes and lowered him into the tank. Harper saw the fluid was thick, like a gel. It surrounded his body, and they rested his head on a small ledge that kept his mouth above the fluid.

"What is it?" Harper asked.

"A regenerative gel," Saff said. "It heals just about anything, but it's expensive as hell. We're lucky to have three regen tanks."

One of the Hermia leaned over, running some sort of scanner over Raiden's form.

"He'll be okay." Harper wasn't sure if her words were a question or a statement.

Saff slid an arm along her shoulders. "Of course, he will. He's Raiden."

Harper swallowed. She wondered if Saff heard the tremor in her own voice.

Then the healer turned and smiled. "The poison is working its way out of his system. Once he finishes in the regen tank, he will be fine."

The tension in the room dropped. She saw Thorin run a hand over his head and Galen's shoulders relax. Kace bumped a shoulder against Saff's.

"Everybody get some rest," Galen said.

As the others shuffled out, Harper didn't move. When Galen stepped in front of her, she lifted her chin. "I'm not leaving him."

"He's in a regenerative coma. He won't wake for a while."

She looked at Raiden. His eyes were closed now, his muscles relaxed. "I don't care."

Galen stared at her face for a moment before he finally nodded and left.

Eventually, the medical team dimmed the lights. Harper dragged a chair over to Raiden's tank and sat down. She released a strained breath. Somehow, this big, alpha gladiator had slipped under her guard.

The hours ticked by as she sat and watched him. She was vaguely aware of Galen checking on her and Saff bringing her something to eat. Soon, the medical staff reappeared and transferred his now-healed body to a regular bed.

"He will sleep for a few more hours yet," one healer told her.

Harper nodded. He was breathing deeply and evenly. Because she needed the contact, she crawled into the bed beside him, curling up against his chest.

She brushed the hair off his face. Damn the Thraxians. They'd taken so much from her, and they were still trying to take the last few things she really cared about.

Exhausted, she pressed her face to his chest. His heart was a steady beat under her ear. Part of her wanted to tell Raiden not to risk his life for her, for Regan.

But she knew her gladiator had a heart of gold, even if he kept it buried under the macho alpha male and the tattoos.

"I see you," she murmured.

She closed her eyes and fell asleep.

Chapter Fourteen

Raiden woke slowly. His skin felt sticky, and he knew what that meant. He'd been in a regen tank.

Draking Thraxians. He shifted slightly, testing his limbs, and felt a warm weight pressed to his side and chest. He frowned, moving his arm. Nothing hurt.

He realized the weight was a woman. *Harper.*

He tried to move and she stirred. Her hand smoothed over his chest.

"Take it easy," she murmured.

He looked down, saw her dark hair spilling across his skin. He liked seeing it like that.

She sat up, reaching over to the side table beside the medical bunk. When she moved to swing her legs off the bed, he gripped her hip. "No."

She looked at him and then nodded. She handed him a cup filled with a blue liquid.

"The healers left this for you." She waited until he took it. "Drink up."

Raiden quickly tossed it back, and grimaced. It never tasted good but he knew it would give him an energy boost.

He reached out, wrapping her hair around his hand.

"Raiden—"

He rolled her beneath him, pinning her down. "I give the orders."

She rolled her eyes. "I'm trying to help you."

"You jumped into the arena."

Her eyes turned cautious. *Yeah, you should be nervous.*

"Yes. And Galen's already chewed me out about it. The match was already forfeited because of the poison—"

"I don't give two draks about the match. You were unprepared. No armor, no warmup, an unfamiliar weapon."

"The Thraxian fighters were going after you. One had gotten past Thorin and the others—"

"It doesn't matter. You *do not* risk yourself. You never go into the arena unprepared."

"I should have let them kill you?" Her voice had risen.

"You should have stayed safe."

"I'm alive." Her blue-gray eyes stared at him, spitting fire. "You almost died!"

She'd been worried about him. Raiden knew he had friends, good friends. He could always count on Thorin and the others to watch his back in the arena.

But it had been years since anyone had worried about him like Harper. Hell, maybe since he'd been a boy.

She pulled away and stood stiffly beside the bed. "The healer said once you were awake you could return to your room. They've organized food to be delivered, and they left this." She grabbed a small vial of oil. "They said it needed to be massaged into the site of your wound."

He eyed the stubborn line of her jaw. "Fine. I'll need your help to get to my room." He pushed the blankets off and stood.

Her gaze slipped down his naked body. "You can't walk back to your room like that."

"Why not? No one will be awake this early."

"Raiden—"

"Are you shy now? You've seen my body before. You've had my cock in your mouth, and in—"

"Raiden." She muttered under her breath. "Fine." She jammed her shoulder into his side. "Let's go."

Raiden was fine, completely healed, but he let her take some of his weight and help him into the corridor.

It was still early and, as he'd predicted, everyone was still in bed. They moved through the empty living area and into his room.

Once she helped him onto the bed, she flicked a sheet over his hips. He watched her, liking the way she bustled around him. For the first time in a long time, someone truly cared about his needs. Yes, his friends cared, they trusted each other with their lives, but none of them fretted over his wounds or plumped the pillows behind his head.

Some of his anger leaked away. She cared, but Thorin was right. Harper would never let Raiden lock her away to keep her safe and she would never blindly follow his orders.

She wouldn't be a sweet, simple woman there to just cater to his needs. She would be a warrior queen, who would stand by his side, no matter what.

And he realized that was why he was so drawn to her.

The tray of food had been delivered, and sat nearby. As he stuffed another pillow behind his back, she brought the tray over and set it down beside him.

"Eat," she said.

The plates were filled with his favorite foods. There was also a steaming cup of Aurelian *lat*.

He took a sip, savoring the bitter flavor. Harper leaned forward and sniffed the air. "That smells like coffee."

"It is from Aurelia and very expensive." He held it out for her and she took a small sip. Her eyes opened wide.

"Holy cow, that's strong."

With a smile, he drank the rest of it in a single gulp. He was going to need the energy.

She was eyeing him warily. "You aren't angry anymore."

"No."

"Why?"

"Because I was being an overbearing ass."

She blinked. "Nice of you to admit that."

He leaned back. "I seem to recall you have to tend to my wound."

She held the vial up and Raiden snatched some small *liven* nuts from the tray. He popped one into his mouth. "Go ahead." But he was planning to have some fun. He tossed the sheet off and slid one arm beneath his head.

Her gaze slid down his body, her cheeks turning a little pink. He felt his cock stir.

"I think you can leave the sheet over your bottom half," she said primly. "Your injury is on your chest."

"Nope." He leaned back, baring his chest more. "Put the oil on."

With a shake of her head, she got close, her knees pressed against his hips. She tipped some of the clear oil on her hand and gingerly started to rub it on his shoulder and chest. He glanced at his wound, noting that, other than a red mark on his skin, there was no sign that he'd been struck by the spear. When he looked up, he smiled. She was looking down his body again, her gaze no doubt watching his cock rise up toward his belly.

The heat in her cheeks deepened. It was such a contradiction to see such a tough warrior who could also blush like a virgin.

"Harder, Harper."

She tipped the vial again, and started rubbing it on his skin in long strokes. She moved down his chest, kneading. Damn, he enjoyed her touch.

"Lower," he murmured.

She raised a brow. "I don't think you were injured down there." But her hands traced over the ridges of his abdomen. It wasn't long before he saw her lips were parted and her breathing was just a little fast.

Desire grew, like music growing louder. It wasn't just what she looked like. He liked everything she did—her opinions, her courage. It was that bravery he saw in the arena, and her dedication to her friends.

His cock was hard, throbbing. Her gaze dropped to it again and she bit her lip. Seeing those white teeth sink into the plump skin broke the last of his control. He reached up, gripped the neck of her shirt and tore it open.

She gasped, the small vial dropping onto the bed. He pushed her back onto the covers, tore off the band covering her breasts, and snatched up the vial. He upended the contents on her breasts and belly.

"Raiden, you were hurt—"

"Not anymore." He ran his hands through the oil, making her skin slick. He cupped her breasts. "You won't risk yourself again."

She bucked against him. "Not that again. I don't take orders, either, gladiator."

"You will." He thumbed her nipples, tweaking them between his fingers.

She arched into his touch. "No, I won't. I'm a gladiator now. Risk is a part of the arena."

One part of him hated knowing she'd have to fight, but another more primal part of him was thrilled to hear her acknowledge her life here. Their life.

He gripped her, lifting her up as he dropped onto his back again. He settled her on his thighs and slid his hands down her belly. "If you won't listen to me, then I'll just have to take what I want."

Again, he saw her breath hitch, her back arch. Yes, his sweet little gladiator liked it when he got bossy, even if she wouldn't admit it. God, she had the prettiest breasts.

He slid his hands down between her thighs. She made a husky sound as he brushed over her clit, and then he thrust a finger inside her tight warmth.

"Yes." She rode his hand and thigh.

"Let me see your surrender, little gladiator."

***

Harper had her face pressed against the covers, her ass in the air, as Raiden pounded into her roughly from behind.

She moaned, her hands twisting in the furs. "Yes, Raiden. More."

His hands dug into her hips. "You take everything I give you and still want more."

"More."

He hammered into her ruthlessly. The sound of flesh hitting flesh filled the room. "You're so tight, Harper. I want you to come now."

"Too much." She was thrusting back against him, riding the bright edge of orgasm.

His hands reached under, even as he continued to drive into her tight body. A flick on her oversensitive clit and she came with a hoarse cry.

Her orgasm triggered his, and she felt the hard dig of his fingers as he roared, his release jetting inside her.

They both collapsed on the large bed. Raiden just barely managed to stop his crushing weight from landing on her.

"I can't move," Harper moaned.

Raiden made a noise that rumbled through his chest. She felt his big hand smooth over her ass. "Not sure what I like best."

She turned her head to look at him. "What do you mean?"

It was nice to see the smile on his lips. His face looked almost relaxed. Or as relaxed as she guessed Raiden could be. "Your mouth on my cock or my cock in that tight pussy of yours."

She rolled her eyes and laughed. "Raiden."

He pulled her in close, rearranging her so her back was plastered against his chest. Then he stroked her hair.

She sighed. "How can I feel so good when I know my friends are in trouble?"

"We will have them free soon."

"How many people have you freed from the arena?"

He tensed slightly beside her. "I don't keep count."

"Yes, you do. I bet their faces are burned into your brain." She was quiet for a second. "You couldn't save your people, so you're making up for it in the arena, one slave at a time."

"Harper."

She recognized his "I don't want to talk about it" voice. "Raiden, I—"

With a growl, he leaped off the bed and scooped her up into his arms. He strode toward the balcony off his room and stepped outside.

She squeaked, gripping his shoulders. "Raiden, we're naked."

He ignored her, and moved along the long, narrow balcony. It offered a sweeping view of the city. At the end, she could see a small circular bathing pool built-in to the balcony. Steam rose off it and it was just big enough for two.

Her eyebrows went up. "A gladiator hot tub?"

"I don't know what a hot tub is, but I'm planning to enjoy a soak with you."

He stepped into the pool and sat down on a ledge under the water. As Harper followed him in, the warm water moved around her skin, and she moaned. It felt so good.

"That's the same sound you make when my cock is moving inside you."

Damn, she liked when her gladiator talked dirty. She spun around in his arms so that she was straddling his lap. For a second, she was caught by that rugged face, those intense eyes. He was a man that you could look at, see in the arena, and make a judgment about. It would be easy just to see the tattooed, bronze skin and the battle-scarred muscles, and never get to know what was really beneath that.

Under her bottom, she felt his swelling cock. She moved against him, tormenting them both.

He groaned, his hand slipping into the water to find her clit. He played with it, rubbing, circling and pinching.

She bit her lip. "You're obsessed."

"I am." He surged out of the water and sat on the edge of the tub, Harper still balanced on his lap. He pushed her thighs apart. "Put me inside you."

Again with that deep voice of command. Maybe princes had it bred into them. She reached down and gripped his cock, running her fingers over the thick head.

"Harper," he growled.

She brought it to the folds between her legs. Then she sank down, absorbing those hard inches into her body. He was big and he'd taken her many times, but she still felt an uncomfortable stretch as he moved deep inside her.

His fingers gripped her hips and he groaned.

Gently, she started to ride him. But soon her pace increased, a fire igniting inside her. He pressed his face to her breasts, nipping and licking at them.

Wild spasms of pleasure started rippling through her, and she knew she was close.

"Look in my eyes, Harper."

Their gazes locked, and she felt a shiver race over her skin, despite the heat they were generating. He bumped his hips up, slamming her down at the same time.

Her release hit like a wave. It rolled through her and she arched into him, her body squeezing on his cock.

He hissed out a curse she didn't recognize, then

she heard his masculine cry. A raw, primal sound that made her smile.

Chapter Fifteen

Raiden liked this picture. He stared at Harper, sitting in the middle of his bed, wearing only one of his shirts. Her long legs were tucked beneath her, and she was eating off the plate of food that he'd had delivered.

On the vid-screen beside the bed, she was watching information on different worlds in the sector. She was munching and listening to everything intently. Absorbing all the information.

He liked seeing her there, amongst his things.

He'd never shared his space with a woman. Usually, he fucked them and sent them on their way.

Suddenly, he heard a familiar word coming from the screen, and his muscles tensed.

"The former world of Aurelia," a woman was saying. He turned to look at the screen, and saw an image of the beautiful blue-green planet that once was his home world.

"Raiden, I'm sorry." Harper came up on her knees, reaching for the control to turn off the screen.

"No." He pressed a hand over hers, coming to sit down on the edge of the bed.

He kept his gaze on the screen, watching as it started to flash through images of the planet's beautiful scenery. Harper moved up behind him, wrapping her body around his. Quietly, they watched it together—the scenery, the cities, the palace.

A bittersweet ache filled his chest. So many memories played through his head. Memories he hadn't let himself think about for a very long time.

"I can't believe you're royalty." She leaned into him. "Here I am, practically naked with a prince."

"Former prince." He saw a beautifully landscaped garden and courtyard. In the distance, the royal palace rose up, majestic and awe-inspiring. "I played there as a boy."

The image changed, and this time, he saw a wide waterfall splashing down into a large blue pool of water. A reluctant smile tugged on his lips. It was near their summer palace. "I used to jump from the top of that waterfall and scare my sister."

Harper rested her cheek against his back, her arms tightening on him. He reached up and pressed his hands around hers.

The next image was of a beautiful sprawl of buildings made of a luminous cream stone, sitting at the base of the jungle-covered mountain. "Our summer palace. That's where I rode my first dragon."

"Dragon?" Her voice was shocked.

"It's a rite of passage for an Aurelian boy."

"Dragon." She said it like she couldn't quite process it.

More images flicked on the screen, showing the lush beauty of his homeworld.

"It's beautiful, Raiden."

"It was." And for the first time, he let himself remember the good times. For so long, when he'd thought of his planet, he'd only thought of the bad. He remembered his parents—how much they'd loved each other. He remembered Naida's laughter. She'd always been running and laughing.

With Harper by his side, he could recall those beautiful places of his planet, and the hauntingly familiar faces of his family, without the usual recurring pain.

Finally, the images changed, and the program moved on to a new planet. He was sorry that there were no images of Earth for him to see. So instead, he turned to face her. "Tell me about your planet?"

"It had its beautiful scenery as well. Breathtaking protected forests, large oceans that we almost destroyed, but luckily we wised up in time. Busy cities with people living on top of each other, tall buildings rising into the sky. Wild, open deserts covered in huge dunes of sand." A faint smile played on her lips. "I guess I never really appreciated it enough. When the opportunity came to go to space, I took it."

Raiden detected more beneath her words. "Tell me about your sister."

Harper let out a long, shaky breath. "My parents were hard workers, but they were also gamblers. They fed us, but they also spent almost every cent they earned in casinos."

"I see that happen here as well," he said. "People come for a visit, a little walk on the wild side. And leave with nothing."

Harper nodded. "My parents died in a vehicle accident when I was seventeen and left us with nothing. I managed to gain custody of Brianna, and without many options for work, I joined the police force. I also took an extra job, working nights and on my days off to provide for my sister. It left her alone a lot."

The quiet held a wealth of pain. He wrapped his fingers around hers.

"She ended up connecting with the wrong crowd. She was young and angry, and got into drugs."

He sensed an old frustration and sadness. "I have seen many here in the arena succumb to forbidden substances. To wash away the pain and not face their reality."

She nodded. "But it doesn't really make reality go away. I think my parents did the same thing with their gambling. While they did it, they could forget their lives. Neither of them liked their jobs, and they complained bitterly that they could never get ahead. But neither of them did anything to change, to go after what they wanted." She sighed. "That was too much hard work, so instead they blamed everyone else, and buried their heads in the sand."

"You are not like your family."

"I loved them so much, even when they disappointed me. I'd lost my parents and then I lost Brianna to her addiction. I got her into a special place where she could be rehabilitated, a really good center that almost bankrupted me. But she didn't want to get better. It didn't matter how much I wanted it for her, it wasn't enough."

"People must want to help themselves, first." He thought of his younger self and Thorin, landing in the arena, angry and wild.

"I know. All I could do was watch her spiral out of control."

"She didn't make it?"

"No, she didn't. I couldn't save her. She overdosed on a filthy floor, in a dirty, abandoned building just blocks away from our apartment. Three days after her funeral, I joined the Space Marines, and ended up at the space station."

"So you went to protect other people, because you hadn't been able to protect your own."

She lifted a shoulder. "A gladiator and a counselor?"

He tugged on her hair. "And now, you'll save Regan and Rory as well."

Harper pushed away and jumped to her feet. "I'll save them because it's the right thing to do. It's not some misguided attempt at atoning for my sister's death."

Raiden just watched her.

She threw out a hand. "Don't look at me like that."

"What do you want, Harper?"

"I want Regan back. I want her and Rory safe."

"No. I mean for you. What do you want for Harper?"

She spun away from him, wrapping her arms around her middle. “What does it matter? I’m a slave, a gladiator, with no way to get back to my planet. And not even a home to go back to.”

Raiden came up behind her, slipping his arms around her. He gripped her chin, and forced her to meet his gaze. “You are not alone.”

The anger leaked from her face, her features softening. “I was always alone before, even when my family was alive.”

A strong surge of emotion stormed through Raiden. “I need my cock in you.”

“Raiden—”

He scooped her up, carrying her a few steps to the table near the window. He set her on the edge, shoving her shirt up over her breasts. Desire was like a raging beast inside him. One that didn’t want to be controlled. It wanted them joined, wanted to claim her—hard.

He spread her legs and shoved his loose trousers down. His cock sprung free. He circled it, pumped it once, then rubbed the thick, mushroom head of it against her damp folds. “Watch.”

She was breathing heavily now, her palms pressed to the slick surface of the table. But she did as he commanded, her gaze locked between them.

Raiden pushed his cock into her small, but willing body. It amazed him every time that she could take him. Her small moan echoed around them, her body stretching to accept him.

Then he slammed all the way inside her. She wrapped her arms around him, calling out his name. This time he kept his rhythm slow, steady. Her nails dug into his shoulders.

She felt hot, tight, better than anything.

Harper felt like home.

***

As they walked into the living area, everyone turned to look at Harper and Raiden. There was an uncomfortable moment of silence, before they all started clapping and cheering.

Harper tried to hide her smile.

Raiden's arm tightened on Harper's shoulder. "Enough," he growled.

Thorin came over, his hands pressed together. "Thank you, Harper. For putting him and us out of his misery."

Raiden swung a fist toward his friend, but Thorin ducked, laughing.

"You're welcome, Thorin," Harper said. "But I have to say that the pleasure was all mine."

More hoots.

Saff came over, holding out a drink that had steam coming off the top of it. "This is my thank you."

Harper accepted it. "What is it?"

Saff paused. "You probably don't want to know. Just enjoy it. I promise it tastes good."

Harper took a sip and found that it did taste good. It tasted very similar to hot chocolate, and almost as good as Raiden's *lat* drink. "Thanks. What is it?"

"It's called *ocla*." Saff waggled her eyebrows. "It is worth more credits than I make in a month. It was a gift from an admirer."

Raiden led her over to some padded seats. He dropped down, and tugged her beside him. She leaned into him, and smiled. It had been a long time since she'd just relaxed and enjoyed other people's company. Even on the space station, she'd tried to hold herself apart, stop from connecting with people.

God, she and Raiden were a real pair.

Thorin was talking to Raiden, holding his attention, but her gladiator was still touching her. He was running his hand up and down her arm.

She saw Nero on the other side of the room, sitting at the table, sharpening knives. She shook her head. The man never took a break and relaxed. Lore was spinning some small metal balls above his palm. How they stayed in the air, she didn't know. Kace was steadily eating a mound of food.

"So," Thorin said. "The House of Thrax got a verbal warning for that little poison stunt."

"A verbal warning? No more than a slap on the wrist?" Harper straightened, almost spilling her drink. "That's it?"

Thorin frowned. "A slap on the wrist?"

"An Earth saying," she said with a wave of her hand.

"As long as no one dies, the 'authorities' around here don't really care," Raiden said. "Whatever keeps the money rolling in." He looked around the room. "Everyone ready for another fight tonight?"

"Hell, yeah."

"Bring it."

"And if we win tonight, we get Regan back, right?" Harper set her cup down.

"Yes."

"But what about Rory?" Rory's beaten but defiant face flashed behind Harper's eyes.

Raiden's face grew serious. "I doubt the Thraxians will let her go as well."

Harper's stomach went tight.

He gripped her chin. "But we won't stop trying. We'll have to fight more battles."

Risk getting hurt. For her and her friends.

"It's what we do," he reminded her. "And I have no qualms about beating on the Thraxians."

But she heard the serious tone in his voice. The Thraxians knew Harper would want her friends back…and knowing that, they'd likely play games. Combined with Raiden's need for revenge…it was a bad combination.

Helplessness. She hated it. She'd felt the same as she'd watched her sister waste her life away. She stood and moved over to the large windows, staring up at the twin suns.

She stared blindly at the ancient city in the distance, and the giant golden orbs in the sky. She felt a rush of sadness and thought of San Diego, her small apartment, and Earth's smaller sun. She used to love watching the sun setting into the Pacific Ocean. But it was a distant sadness, the bittersweet thoughts of things that had passed.

"Harper?"

Raiden's granite body pressed into her back. She leaned into his hard strength, resting her head against his chest. "After my sister died, it took some time, but I realized life goes on. It doesn't matter what you've faced, what matters is what you do despite it." She turned into her gladiator and traced some of the tattoos on his chest. She didn't think he'd quite learned that lesson yet. She knew his past was still a huge driver for him finding his vengeance.

She wondered if vengeance would really give him the peace he sought.

If she was honest, she'd been doing a crappy job of living after she'd lost Brianna. She'd thrown herself into her work, as far from Earth as she could get. She'd been going through the motions, but she hadn't really been living.

Maybe it was time to change that? Even if she was on an outer-rim alien planet. Even if home was a wild, gladiatorial arena, and her life now revolved around that arena, and the gladiator standing in front of her.

She moved her fingers over another of his tattoos in a gentle caress.

"Quit doing that, or you'll end up back in my bed." His voice was deep and husky.

She smiled. "What's this say?"

"It talks of my oath to my people and my planet. My promise to lead them, protect them, and put them first."

His tone was blank, but she felt his sorrow. Sympathy was a sharp pain inside her. She leaned forward and pressed a kiss to his chest.

He growled, the sound vibrating under her lips. Suddenly, there was a scuffle from the doorway.

"Hey, look what I found skulking around outside." Thorin was dangling a small kid a meter off the ground.

The boy looked half-starved, and was busy kicking and cursing to get free.

"Put me down! I have a message for the woman from Earth."

Harper froze, and felt Raiden's body go tense beside her. She strode forward. "That's me."

Thorin let the boy down. He was wearing simple clothes that were ragged and stained with dirt. He looked her up and down with a gaze that seemed far too old for such a young person. "You're small."

She rolled her eyes. "So everyone tells me." She snatched up a bread roll from the table, and held it out. "What do you have for me?"

He eyed the roll like a thief eyeing diamonds. Quick as a flash, he snatched the bread and shoved a piece of paper at her. As the boy devoured the bread, she opened the note.

She frowned. This time, the message on it was in an illegible alien scrawl. "I can't read it."

Raiden looked over her shoulder. As his gaze moved over the text, his face darkened.

Harper felt her stomach go tight. "Tell me."

"It could be another trap—"

"Tell me," she said again.

"It says that Regan is going to be moved." He released a breath. "That she's going to be sold to off-world slavers."

"What?" A horrified whisper. "But the Thraxian imperator agreed she'd be part of the fight tonight. How can he go back on his word?"

"Because he's Thraxian."

"It sounds like another trap," Thorin said.

"But what if it's not?" Harper turned to Raiden. "What if I don't do anything, and she's gone? Gone forever."

"It's true," the kid said, lifting his dirt-streaked face. "And it's not just her being sold. The other Earth woman with her is being sold, too."

Chapter Sixteen

Raiden strapped on his leather harness, looking at the map of the House of Thrax spread out on the table. He pressed his finger to one point. "We'll go in here."

"Or here." Thorin pointed to another location.

Raiden nodded. "That's a good option, too. We'll keep it as a backup, if we need it."

"Let's hope we don't need it," Saff murmured.

"We need to get in there, get the women, and get out without anyone seeing us," Raiden said. "Or at least without anyone being able to identify us."

Around him, his gladiators all wore unrelieved black and had black masks that would cover the top half of their faces dangling around their necks. Tonight, his cloak was pure black. Lore was fiddling with some things he planned to bring on the mission. Lore's tricks had gotten them out of some tight spots before. Nero was silent and menacing, while Kace was calm and focused.

He saw Harper watching them. She'd locked down her worry for now, but he could still it see in her eyes.

"You've done this before," she said.

He raised a brow.

"You've snuck in and freed people before. From the other gladiator houses."

He looked at his team and then back to his woman. "Yes. When Galen hasn't been able to negotiate them as a prize in the arena, we go in and free them."

"I'm guessing that's not legal."

There were chuckles from all around them. "A lot of stuff isn't legal out here on the rim," Thorin said.

"No one cares too much about rules out here," Raiden said. "But people can extract their own brutal payback. It's best we aren't caught."

Harper pulled in a deep breath, and he grabbed her hands, smoothing his fingers over her wrists.

"And if we're caught?"

"We die."

She moved into him, went up on her toes, and kissed him. "You're a good man, Raiden."

"Hey," Thorin complained. "I'm risking my ass, too. Where's my kiss?"

Harper's eyes stayed on Raiden. "You're a good leader. You would've been an amazing king."

Raiden felt a hit of warmth in his chest. "Put your mask on. We need to go."

All of them finished getting ready and moved into the corridor. It was late, everything wreathed in darkness. Galen met them, his face set. "Be careful."

Raiden nodded. Galen looked like he wanted to say something else. "I know you want to come, but we can't risk it. If we're caught, someone has to ensure the House of Galen still stands."

A muscle in Galen's jaw ticked but he nodded. "Good fighting."

Raiden made sure Harper stayed between him and Thorin, as they moved through the maze of tunnels. A few times they had to change their route to avoid the guard patrols that wandered the arena at night.

Raiden had hoped their luck would hold, but as they moved down the larger tunnel leading to the House of Thrax, the sound of guards talking ahead of them caught his ear.

Damn. Raiden looked around. There was nowhere to hide. No side tunnels or doorways.

He lifted his hand and waved at the rest of his team. They pulled back, melting into what shadows they could find.

What he needed was a distraction to keep the guards from looking too closely at where his gladiators were poorly hidden. He grabbed Harper and pushed her up against the rock wall. She made a muffled squeak, her gaze on his, but she didn't protest.

He wrapped her legs around his hips and pressed his mouth close to hers. "Make it look good." He started moving his hips against hers like he was fucking her.

She got into their little deception quickly. She started moaning loudly, her hands clamping on his head.

The guards neared and Raiden could hear them chuckling.

"Man, wish I could find myself something like that," one said in a deep voice.

Raiden ground himself against Harper, willing the guards to keep moving. Thankfully, they passed the tunnel entrance and kept going.

Raiden went still and pressed his face against Harper's hair. "Damn."

"What?" she whispered.

"I've got a hard-on."

She let out a little surprised laugh, her legs dropping from around his waist.

Once she was steady on her feet and he had his body back under control, he lifted his hand and gestured for the rest of them to follow.

They kept going, until they reached the grate that had been marked on the map. The rusted metal covered an old tunnel that had been decommissioned.

He waved a hand and Saff moved forward, pulling a small tool off her belt. She started loosening the thick metal bolts holding the grate in place.

When Saff nodded, Kace and Thorin shifted the heavy grate to the side, uncovering the yawning darkness of the dank tunnel. It was older and smaller than the active tunnels.

"Careful," Raiden warned them. "It's old. It probably had a cave in or other damage for it to have been closed down."

He went first. He had to stoop over as it wasn't tall enough for him. It was fine for Harper who moved quietly behind him. The rest of his team followed. After Nero stepped in, Kace and Thorin slid the grate back mostly into place in order to avoid raising suspicion.

They moved through the thick blackness, stepping carefully over an area where some chunks of rock had fallen from the roof. Soon, they reached another grate.

Saff squeezed forward with her tool, and soon Raiden slowly and quietly moved it to the side. He was careful not to make a sound and alert any Thraxian guards.

They all stepped out into the cell area of the House of Thrax.

Everything was very quiet.

Raiden felt the hairs on the back of his neck rise. He hated when things were so quiet. Dim lanterns spaced irregularly on the walls gave off a faint glow.

But it wasn't going to stop him from rescuing Harper's friends.

***

Harper crept forward silently, searching through the gloom to look in the cells. She saw bodies curled up on the hard stone floors.

God, no one deserved this. She wanted to save everybody, even though she knew she couldn't.

They reached the cells where she'd seen her friends before. She touched the bars, searching each enclosure.

They were empty.

Dammit. Anxiety nipped at her with sharp teeth. Had they been moved already? Was she too late?

She looked at Raiden and shook her head. His hand touched her cheek briefly, and she took strength from the touch. He waved his hand and they kept moving.

Suddenly, she tripped over something near her foot. She flung her arms out and managed to stay on her feet. What the hell? The dim light of the lanterns glimmered on a wire stretched across the corridor.

Oh, no. There was a whooshing sound from above, and something dropped down on her.

It was a net. As she raised her hands to protect herself, she heard Raiden and the others cursing. Something sizzled against her skin, burning, and the metallic ropes were beginning to glow as they heated up.

She wriggled, fighting to get free, trying to keep the net from touching her skin in any one spot for too long, but the more she moved, the more the net tightened around her.

Movement. Raiden appeared, a stripe of a burn on his cheek, and cut through the ropes with his sword. As the net fell to the ground, glowing red, she shuddered.

"Are you okay?" he asked.

She checked her arms, found a few minor burns, but nothing bad. She nodded.

"That would have triggered an alarm," he said. "They'll be coming." He waved to the others. Saff was helping Kace to his feet. The gladiator had a bad burn across his chest. The rope had burned through his shirt. Nero, Thorin and Lore loomed in the darkness.

"We can't leave Regan and Rory," Harper said, her tone resolute.

"We don't have much time. I won't let the Thraxians take you again."

"I hear guards incoming," Thorin said, lifting his axe.

"I suggest we hide," Lore said. He held something on his palm. "Everyone get behind me."

They all huddled behind the lanky gladiator. Raiden pulled Harper close to his side. Lore touched something and she saw a faint blue shimmer appear. It spread out in front of them.

"What is it, magic man?" Saff whispered.

"If it works, then the incoming guards will just see a projection of the rock wall behind us."

"*If* it works?" Raiden said.

Lore shrugged. "I haven't had a chance to test it."

Harper tried to calm her racing heartbeat. Then, the Thraxian guards appeared. She slipped her hand in Raiden's, squeezing tightly.

All the gladiators were tense. She knew this kind of operation went against their nature. They all liked action, not hiding and waiting.

A guard glanced their way, but apparently didn't see anything wrong. They were all crouched now, studying the nets. A few of the prisoners stood at the cell bars, watching sullenly. God, she hoped none of them would do anything to cause trouble. If they gave them away…

After a few more minutes, she could tell that the guards had completely relaxed.

"These nets are worthless," one guard growled.

"You're right, they never work properly." Another guard nodded in agreement.

"Let's go," the first guard said, kicking the nets against the wall. "Nothing down here worth worrying about."

That was their first mistake.

"Let's see if the guards can tell us where the women are," Raiden murmured almost soundlessly. "Ready?"

Raiden lifted his hand, then brought it down in a hard slash.

Before Harper could draw her swords, Lore dropped the illusion, and the gladiators rushed forward. The bewildered guards barely had time to draw their weapons before the gladiators attacked them. Metal rang on metal.

Unlike their fighting style in the arena, this time, the gladiators fought silently, using swift, efficient, and lethal moves. Thorin still packed a huge punch, but there were no shouts or cheers. Kace was quiet, working with the drive of a military commander. Saff and Nero took down their opponents as quickly as they could, while Lore was completely devoid of showmanship and tricks, just attacking with dangerous skill.

And Raiden was Raiden. He was no different whether he was fighting in the arena, or fighting in the darkness of a secret mission. He did the job and was deadly.

They showed no mercy, and Raiden only kept one guard alive. He pressed the blade of his sword to the alien's throat, the inscriptions on it glowing softly. "Where are the women from Earth?"

The guard made a gurgling sound.

Raiden shoved the blade harder into the Thraxian's tough skin. "Where?"

"Torture cells," the alien coughed out.

Torture cells? Harper felt her stomach drop away.

Raiden removed his sword and slammed his elbow down into the guard's face. He slumped to the floor.

"This way." Raiden waved them down another tunnel.

Harper moved in close, falling in behind Raiden.

"The House of Thrax has some cells they use for interrogation and torture, as well as solitary confinement."

"If they've hurt them..." Harper said, her tone fierce.

"Likely the Thraxians were just keeping them separated from the general population before transfer."

Ahead, she saw a dim glow of light. A single Thraxian guard was sitting on a stool in front of a door, looking bored.

"Mine," she said.

Raiden looked down at her and smiled. He waved her forward.

Harper moved quickly, raising her swords. The guard spotted her at the last second, surging to his feet. But he was too late.

Harper sliced one sword across his belly and sunk her second blade into his shoulder. Blood splattered the rock floor. He cried out and she leaped on him, riding him to the ground.

When she stood, the others were by her side. She turned to face the door. It had a small metal grate built into the top of it.

"Who's there?" a quiet whisper.

Harper hurried to the door. "Regan? I'm here."

A slim hand gripped the grate, a face appearing from the shadows.

Harper froze. The woman looked almost human, but had pointed ears and slits on her forehead.

"Your friends are gone," the woman said.

Chapter Seventeen

Raiden watched Thorin wrench the door open. The Gallian woman stumbled out.

Harper shifted impatiently. "Do you know where Regan and Rory are?"

The woman's face fell. "They took them. The one called Rory was taken to another location. She's to be sold to someone local. The other, Regan…they took her not long ago. They said something about a ship."

Harper's hands tightened on the woman. "I have to find them."

Raiden frowned. "We can't go after both."

Harper's face twisted with the agony of her decision. "If the ship leaves the planet—"

He nodded. "We'll find Rory after we get Regan."

"We have to move. It won't be long before the Thraxians notice something is wrong," Thorin said. "We've got to go now."

Raiden nodded, touching Harper's shoulder. "Come."

"Please," the Gallian woman whispered. "Take me with you."

"What's your name?"

"Darla."

"Saff," Harper said quietly. "Can you get Darla back to the House of Galen?"

Saff nodded, turning to the woman. "Of course." The female gladiator's gaze flicked up to Raiden's. He knew she'd hate to miss a fight, but he knew she was just as protective of those who were weaker.

He looked at Kace. "Go with them. Stay safe." The gladiator nodded.

When they reached the exit tunnel, Harper turned to Darla. "These are my friends, Saff and Kace. You need to go with them. They'll get you somewhere safe."

"Where?" the woman asked.

"To the House of Galen."

Darla blanched, taking a step back. "Another gladiator house? Where I'll be a prisoner again?"

"No, you won't." Harper shook her head. "I can't explain right now, but I need you to trust me."

Darla looked up at Raiden, standing behind Harper. "He looks at you like he owns you."

Raiden stepped forward. "I would die to protect her."

The woman's mouth dropped open, and she was silent for a moment. "Okay."

Harper's mouth rose in a smile. "Go with Saff and Kace."

Raiden waited until Harper had helped her new friend into the tunnel with the chosen gladiators. He gave his remaining gladiators a nod, and they moved into the tunnel. Raiden took a second to set the grate back in place.

"We need to hurry," Raiden said. "They will have gone to the spaceport."

"Quickest way is through the old town center," Thorin said.

Raiden nodded. They moved fast, and soon snuck out of the arena. As they moved into the darkened streets, he kept his gaze sharp. Kor Magna at night could be a dangerous place. Gangs roamed the streets—former gladiators, wannabe gladiators, people the arena had chewed up and spat out.

They crossed a silent courtyard space, the benches all empty and dark. No lights glowed in the nearby buildings. Soon, they moved back into the narrow twisting streets between the buildings.

Suddenly, a group of dark figures appeared at the end of the alleyway. He muttered a curse. "Keep going," he murmured to his team. He reached up and pulled his mask off.

As they got closer, he could see it was one of the gangs—each one wore an identical red patch on their clothing. They were starting to fan out to ambush the group, when their leader's gaze fell on Raiden.

A second later, the gang backed up, and disappeared into the shadows.

"Thank God for that badass reputation of yours," Harper said.

They kept moving, and soon they emerged from the alleyways in front of a high metal fence.

Beyond the wire, bright lights illuminated the

Kor Magna Spaceport.

There were various spaceships parked on the hard-packed sand. But it was the huge, cigar-shaped, spike-ridden Thraxian ship that dominated the space.

Beside Raiden, Harper stumbled. Something terrible moved across her face.

He gripped her arm. “Harper?”

“It looks exactly like the ship I was on.” Her tone wooden.

He squeezed her arm. “You aren’t on there anymore. You escaped.”

“But I have to go back.”

“No.” He swung her around to face him. “You’re going to save your friend, and this time, you aren’t alone. I’m with you. Every step of the way.”

“I’ve always been alone. Even when my family was alive, they only lived for themselves and their needs. Never for me.”

“I’m here, Harper.”

“Thank you.” She stared back at the ship, then nodded and lifted her chin. “Let’s find Regan.”

***

Harper moved stealthily as she ran along the hull of the ship. Just being near it made her chest tight, but she kept her thoughts focused on Regan.

They found a small side entry port with only a single guard on duty. Raiden took him down without a sound.

As they stepped inside, Harper had to steel

herself. The familiar dark floor and corridor made her shudder.

Raiden took the lead, consulting a small computer screen that projected from his wrist. He'd managed to find a rough map of a Thraxian ship in the House of Galen archives. They were currently heading toward the holding cells.

Then they heard the rumble of voices ahead.

Raiden opened a door into a side room, which was thankfully empty. It looked like some sort of dining area. They all moved inside and pressed against the walls on either side of the door.

The voices got louder, the Thraxians lingering just outside the doorway.

"The new prisoner is being processed. I am not sure what all the fuss is about. There is not much to her."

Harper closed her eyes. *Hold on, Regan.*

"Removing her is a favor to the imperator here. Commander Yoxx wants her settled, and then we will be leaving. We have a slave auction on Yandras II to make."

Harper felt Raiden stiffen beside her. She felt the tension vibrating off him. "What's wrong?" she whispered.

A muscle worked in his jaw. His hands had clenched into hard fists. "Yoxx."

She waited, dread settling in her belly. She heard the Thraxians move off.

"Yoxx was the commander in charge of the assault on Aurelia."

God. She felt a tightness in her chest. She felt all

the others around them go tense. “Raiden—”

He pressed his fists to the wall. “For years, I’ve dreamed of finding him. Years, I’ve imagined driving my sword through him.”

“Raiden.” Thorin’s voice. “This ship is going to launch soon. We have to find Harper’s friend and get out. We don’t have time for Yoxx.”

Harper pressed her hands to Raiden’s chest, bleeding for him.

“Would you let the person responsible for destroying your life get away?”

Thorin’s jaw tightened and he stayed silent.

Harper barely recognized the stark lines of Raiden’s hard face. It was like he wasn’t even seeing them anymore, his thoughts focused on the commander.

Harper caught her fingers against his leathers. “If we lose Regan, she’ll be gone forever. Lost into slavery.”

“He destroyed my planet!”

The raw pain in his voice tore at Harper. She wanted more than anything for him to find the closure he so desperately needed. But she very much doubted he’d find it in vengeance.

“Will killing him bring your planet back?” she asked quietly. “Will it bring your family back?”

“No. But I’ll have my revenge.”

“Please, Raiden. I have to get to Regan. And I need your help to get her out of here.”

He was shaking his head again. “We’ll split up. Thorin, Nero, Lore, go with Harper and find her friend. I will meet you after.”

Harper pulled in a shuddering breath. He was going to leave her. She fought back her emotions. She understood his pain. She understood what it was to lose everything that mattered, but looking at him now, she realized he wasn't even thinking of her. She realized that she wasn't important enough to him.

She understood. This was everything he'd lived for, and it was far more important than a woman from Earth that he'd shared a bed with for a short time. She'd never been important enough to anyone before. Not her parents. Not her sister. Not Raiden.

Harper stepped back. "Of course."

Something in her voice seemed to snap his attention back to her. He frowned. "Harper—"

"It's okay. You've made your choice. Go. Before the ship leaves."

His hands circled her wrists. "I will take care of Yoxx and then I'll be back—"

She lifted her chin. "I need to get to Regan." She gripped his hands, squeezed, then removed them from her skin.

She turned, finding Thorin's gaze. Right now, she needed to focus on Regan and not her bleeding heart. "Ready?"

Harper turned away from the gladiator who'd made her believe in things that didn't exist. Right now, she knew that the only person she could depend on was herself.

She headed out of the room, and back down the corridor in the direction of the cells. She heard the men walking quietly behind her.

"Harper, I'm sorry about Raiden—"

Harper shook her head. "It's fine, Thorin." She ignored the sympathy in his voice and she forced all thoughts of Raiden out of her head. He'd made his decision, and it hadn't been her.

They hurried onward and when she saw the metal-lined corridor, she knew they were getting close.

Suddenly, the lights went out and the corridor was plunged into darkness.

Harper froze, her heart hammering against her ribs. "Do you think they've detected us?"

"Probably." Thorin slapped his axe head against his palm.

Nero gave an unhappy nod.

She nodded grimly. "Then let's keep moving." She gripped the hilt of her swords harder. She didn't care how many Thraxians she had to take down. She wasn't leaving here without Regan.

They moved to the end of the corridor and paused at the junction. "Left or right?"

Thorin studied the map on his wrist. "I think we need to go right—"

A strange coughing echoed in the darkness.

It raised the hairs on Harper's arms. *Shit.* She tried to see through the shadows. What the hell had made that terrible sound?

"Sounds like a Thraxian hunting cat," Lore said.

"I'm guessing they aren't cute and fluffy," Harper said.

"You'd be right."

Then, she saw the shadows move, and a lean,

powerful body slunk out of the darkness. Her muscles froze, and she saw reflective orange eyes looking at her. The creature growled again.

It looked like a black panther, but without the fur. A long, sleek body with huge, clawed paws. It had the same tough skin as the Thraxians, and a set of horns rising up from its large head.

Then, it lifted its head and bared sharp tusks on either side of its teeth-filled jaws.

Scratch that. Not a panther, a sabretooth tiger.

There was movement behind the creature. Three more of the giant, cat-like beasts slunk forward.

Harper swung her swords out in front of her. “Here, kitty kitty.”

She heard Thorin snort. “You have large balls, Earth girl.”

Then the lead creature launched itself forward with a powerful leap.

Thorin’s big body shoved in front of Harper. He gripped the creature, his hands digging into its black skin, and he spun and slammed it into the wall.

Harper heard claws on metal and turned. The other three cats were sprinting forward. Lore and Nero rushed forward to engage.

“Bring it,” she cried.

***

Raiden carefully snuck toward the bridge of the ship. He turned a corner and saw two Thraxians walking toward him.

Silently, he attacked, swinging his sword in a wide arc. Thraxian blood sprayed the walls, and with two more slashes, they were dead.

He kept moving, the heat in his blood fueling him. Yoxx was close. Yoxx was a dead man.

Raiden carefully moved past an open doorway.

"The hunting cats have engaged the intruders."

A second Thraxian gave a deep-throated laugh. "It won't be long until there's nothing left but bones."

Raiden paused. *Drak.* Harper and the others were fighting Thraxian hunting cats. Raiden had faced one in the arena, once. The creatures were strong, bloodthirsty, and enjoyed eating flesh.

Doubt niggled at him. Thorin would protect Harper. Hell, she could protect herself.

Her face drifted into his head. The way she'd looked as he'd left her. The dead look in her eyes.

It was like she'd cut him off.

With a shake of his head, Raiden kept moving. He forced himself to think of his family. His slaughtered mother and father, his violated, dead sister. They'd never had the chance to grow old, and his sister had never had the chance to become who she'd had the potential to be.

They deserved to be avenged. He deserved to spill Yoxx's blood.

But Raiden's steps slowed, his sword dropping to his side. His memories of them were faded. He wondered if wherever they were now, if they cared about vengeance.

The most colorful memories in his head were of

his friends here in the arena. Of his purpose in the arena to save those who shouldn't be there.

Of Harper.

Harper, the small woman who'd gotten under his skin and made him feel so much more. She'd brought him back to life.

And he'd left her.

Just like everyone else in her life had left her.

Drak it all. Raiden turned, and started running back toward her and the others.

As he passed the guard room again, he heard the vicious snarls of the cats. He realized the Thraxians must be watching some sort of security footage.

Then he heard a familiar, deep voice. Thorin. "Run, Harper. Run!"

No. No.

Raiden charged into the room, taking down the unprepared guards with two swift moves. He charged back into the corridor and kept sprinting.

He had to get to Harper.

Chapter Eighteen

Harper's heart was pounding as she scrambled on her hands and knees through a ventilation duct. Thorin had boosted her up into the ceiling. As she moved along it, she was well aware she was leaving a trail of blood behind her.

One cat had scored a hit with its sharp claws, tearing through her leather trousers and gouging her side. She was bleeding, but she didn't think it was too bad. The insane stinging on her side sucked, but she'd live.

God, she hoped that Thorin, Nero, and Lore were okay. The image of Raiden appeared before her eyes, but she slammed down on that thought.

The dense blackness made her feel like she was drowning. Once again, she was alone in the dark. She pushed that disheartening thought away and stopped to look at the wrist map Thorin had shoved at her. It was far too big on her wrist, but she appreciated the faint glow of light. She needed to go a little farther ahead and then climb upward. After that, she'd take another shaft right down to the prison cells.

Ignoring the pain of her bleeding side, she kept crawling. Once she found the vertical vent, she climbed up, pressing her boots to the slick sides and edging her way upward.

Partway up, she paused to catch her breath. She wondered if Raiden had found the commander. Was he okay?

Quit thinking about him, Harper. He left you. She started climbing again.

She climbed out of the vertical shaft and pulled herself into the horizontal section of the duct. She was sweating now and feeling a little shaky. She rested her head against the cool wall, refusing to let the tears come.

Touching her side, she swiped at it with the hem of her shirt, trying to mop up some of the blood.

Then she heard a sound echo through the vent duct.

It sounded like something scraping across the metal. Had someone followed her? The duct was too small for any of the gladiators, or the Thraxians. Even the hunting cats would have a hard time fitting in.

The sound came again, followed by a long, deep rumble that reverberated in the air around her.

A chill ran down her spine. Whatever it was, it wasn't a cat. It was something else.

Shit. She started moving again, scrambling as fast as she could. She came to a crossways and stopped. Which way? Dammit, she'd gotten herself confused. She turned and kept going.

At the next crossways, she knew she was lost. She turned her wrist, studying the map.

Then she heard something else. An animal

breathing. Behind her.

Harper turned, staring into the shadows. She couldn't see a damn thing.

Then slowly a face appeared out of the darkness.

Her chest locked.

This alien was the thing of nightmares. It had a large, triangular-shaped head, with smooth gray skin, and a row of shiny black eyes. It opened its jaws, drool dripping from them.

It moved slowly forward and she saw it had several long legs, it's bottom half making her think of a spider.

It let out a bloodcurdling shriek and rushed forward.

Harper jerked herself backward. She hated to turn her back on it, but she could go faster facing forward. She turned and started crawling.

She heard it coming after her, claws scratching in the metal. It made the deep rumbling sound again that made her stomach turn over.

Ahead, she saw that the duct descended. Harper reached for her remaining sword. She pulled it out, turned. She threw herself backward, sliding wildly downward, like she was on a slide. She held her sword up, ready if the damn alien caught her.

The duct leveled out and she skidded to a halt.

She looked up and saw the creature sliding down the duct toward her. She glanced back behind herself, looking at her options for escape.

Her heart stopped. *No.* It couldn't be.

It was a dead end.

***

Raiden rushed through a corridor and skidded around the corner. Ahead, he saw Thorin battling a hunting cat.

The bodies of several other hunting cats lay sprawled on the floor. Lore stood against one wall, blood running down his arm. His chest was torn up, covered in claw marks. Nero was cleaning off his sword.

"Where's Harper?" Raiden demanded.

Thorin finished the cat and lowered his axe. "See you came to your senses."

"Where is she?"

"I got her into a ventilation duct." He pointed upward. "She was bleeding, and I figured it was the safest place for her, and she could reach her friend faster."

Raiden relaxed a little bit, but he wouldn't be fully satisfied until he saw her with his own eyes. Touched her. "She's heading towards the cells?"

Thorin nodded.

"Then let's find her and get off this damn ship." Together, the four of them moved in the direction of the cells.

They hadn't gone far, when Raiden heard a deep, rasping rumble that echoed through the walls around them. He looked up. The sound was coming from the ventilation system.

Everything inside Raiden went cold. He knew that sound. It was a *nama*. One of the nastiest aliens he'd ever known. They were strictly banned from the arena.

He looked up. "It's in the ducts. It's hunting her."

He took off at a sprint. He followed the noises the creature was making.

Raiden focused on the sound, pushing himself faster and faster. Then he realized the sound was duller. He stopped. "Double back! We moved away from them."

Hold on, Harper. He heard the sounds of a scuffle in the ducts. The *nama* screeched.

"Harper!" he roared.

He moved farther down the corridor. He could hear the sounds of bodies slamming against metal. The *nama* screeched again.

With a roar, Raiden snatched Thorin's axe. He swung it and slammed it against the wall. The panel dented. He swung again and again.

"Stand back."

Raiden didn't want to stop, but he looked at his friend. Thorin ran forward, ramming the wall with his shoulder. He moved back, and Raiden swung the axe at the loosened panel.

The axe tore through the metal.

Raiden shoved the axe back at Thorin, and gripped the ragged metal. Ignoring the sting as razor-sharp edges ripped into his hands, he heaved, pulling it apart. He had to get to Harper.

He tore until the hole was big enough to shove his body through. He pushed inside. "Harper!"

Instantly he saw her. And just beyond her was the *nama*.

She was jabbing her sword at the creature, the stench of its blood filling the tight space.

The single-minded need to protect his woman washed over him. He reached in, grabbed her, and yanked her back.

She cried out, twisting as he pulled her into the corridor, struggling against him.

"Harper! It's me. You're okay." He pulled her away from the wall.

She blinked at him. "Raiden?" She was covered in blood and gore.

"I'm here."

Suddenly, the *nama* rammed out of the hole in the wall, screeching.

Raiden pushed Harper aside, and pulled out his sword. Thorin stormed forward with his axe.

They slashed at the creature, and then Harper joined them, thrusting her sword into the beast's belly.

Stubborn, courageous woman. The *nama* pulled back, writhing. Thick, black blood sprayed over them all.

A second later, the creature fell back into the duct.

Raiden spun, grabbing Harper. "Are you okay?"

Half of her face was covered in blood, and her clothes were soaked with sweat and filth. He cupped her cheeks, forcing her to meet his gaze.

"What are you doing here?" she asked.

When she tried to pull away from him, he held her tight. "I'm making up for my lapse in judgment. Harper, I screwed up. I should never have left you."

Something leaped in her gaze, but she didn't lean into him. Instead, she pulled away, and gave him a small nod. "We can't talk about that now. I need to find Regan."

His jaw tightened, hating that he felt the distance between them. But she was right, and he was going to make things up to her.

"Let's move."

***

They finally reached the holding area.

Harper crept quietly, very conscious of Raiden moving right behind her. The lighting in the area was dim and she peered at the row of cells along one side of the room.

Bile crept into her throat. She took in the regular spacing between the doors, the slim patch of bars letting the jailors look into each cell. Horrific memories rushed forward and she shuddered. Exactly like the cell she'd lived in.

Then, she spotted something ahead in the corridor. Something pale hanging from the ceiling.

She frowned, signaling to the others. She stepped closer and sucked in a shocked breath.

Regan's pale, naked body was chained, dangling in the corridor in front of the cells.

Oh, God. Without thinking, Harper rushed forward. A strong arm circled her waist, holding her in place.

"Let me go—"

Lights clicked on. Going from darkness to bright

light in a flash left Harper blinking.

Then her heart clenched. Behind Regan stood a wall of Thraxians. In the center was a tall Thraxian with an air of authority, his horns larger than those around him. By the way Raiden hissed out a breath, she guessed this was Commander Yoxx.

"You," Raiden breathed.

The commander studied him. "One of the last of the Aurelians."

"Yes," Raiden said. "Because of you and your evil species. I am Prince Raiden Tiago, of the Royal House of Aurelia."

The commander's eyes widened. "The missing crown prince. I always thought you'd died on the planet." The Thraxian shrugged his shoulders. "We sell our services to the highest bidder. Destroying your planet wasn't personal."

"And killing my parents, raping my sister?"

The commander inclined his head, an expression that had to pass for a small smile tugging at his ugly, wide lips. "We're allowed to enjoy what we do."

Raiden lunged forward, and this time it was Harper who blocked him, keeping her body pressed against him.

"Raiden, you need to keep your cool. He's purposely antagonizing you."

She pressed herself against him, hoping to hold him. She turned and looked at the Thraxians.

"You've been using my friends as bait," Harper said. "Toying with us. How does that fit with you just selling your services to the highest bidder? This feels personal."

"We still enjoy a challenge. All of life is a game to fight and win. We worship strength and power and those who wield it." The man's orange gaze settled on Raiden. "And this one causes trouble for the House of Thrax here in the Kor Magna Arena. I figured flushing him out, and taking him down, was a worthy cause." He nodded his head at his guards. "Kill them."

As the Thraxians advanced, Harper looked up at Raiden. "You with me?" She looked at Thorin and Lore. "We need to work as a team to take them all down."

Raiden gave one hard nod. "Together."

Harper drew her sword at the same time as Raiden. His friends flanked them, and they rushed forward.

With single-minded determination, Harper fought. Her sword crashed against the swords of the Thraxians. She heard her gladiators bellowing, fighting with their usual frightening intensity.

As Raiden engaged two Thraxians, keeping their attention on him, she slid in low, slicing at their legs.

She glanced at Regan's still form. Her friend was hurt and in danger. Harper was ready to end this.

"Harper." Raiden gripped her waist. "Ready?"

She nodded, bracing herself. In one swift motion, he tossed her upward. She flew through the air, swung her sword, and took down two Thraxians. Then she was up, leaping, and sliding her legs around the neck of the next Thraxian. She overbalanced him and brought him down. Raiden was waiting to finish him.

"Kill the prisoner," she heard the commander scream. "Take away their reason for fighting."

Harper spun. She saw a Thraxian with an axe heading toward Regan.

No! Harper renewed her fighting. But there were still too many between her and Regan. She wasn't going to be fast enough.

She saw a blur of movement out of the corner of her eye. Thorin! He was closer.

"Thorin! Get to Regan."

The big gladiator looked up. When he saw the Thraxian heading toward Regan, he hefted his own axe and charged forward.

A Thraxian swung at her. Harper ducked and hit back. At the same moment, she saw Commander Yoxx make a run for the door.

"Raiden!" When he caught her gaze, she pointed at the fleeing alien. "Get him."

For a second, Raiden hesitated.

Raiden deserved his closure, and the commander deserved not to leave this place. "Get him! Don't let him escape."

Raiden rushed forward, lifting his sword. The commander pulled his weapon, and she saw the two swords clash with a deafening clang.

Then, a vicious blow hit her legs, behind her knees. Harper fell, slamming into the floor, all air leaving her lungs. She rolled...and saw a very familiar Thraxian standing over her with a large staff.

Scar Face.

She leaped to her feet, swinging her sword. The guard countered with his staff. They traded several blows, each powerful hit shuddering up her arms.

Then he swung again, down low. Harper jumped over it.

Enough. She lunged at him, aiming for his chest.

His heavy staff swung down, not aimed at her sword.

It slammed into her thigh. She felt pain like a hot blade, and she heard the bone snap. She went down with a cry.

The next hit slammed into her ribs. She grunted.

"You were always trouble," Scar Face growled.

She tried to roll, ignoring the burning pain tearing through her body. He slammed the staff down again, on her other leg. This time, she screamed.

Then she heard Raiden's roar. "No!"

Chapter Nineteen

Thorin

Thorin charged toward Harper's small friend. As the alien nearing her raised his axe, Thorin brought his down, slamming into the Thraxian's back.

The big alien shouted and spun. He swung his axe wildly.

Thorin methodically beat the alien back until he slammed into the wall. Another chop of his axe, and the Thraxian slumped to the ground.

Spinning, Thorin moved to free the female. He really hoped that Harper's friend was still alive.

He stopped and blinked.

She'd gotten herself free of her bindings. She stood there, naked, rubbing her bruised wrists.

"You're with Harper?" she asked in a melodious voice.

He nodded. She had the prettiest blue eyes he'd ever seen, in such a small, delicate face.

"Good." She took a step toward him and then collapsed.

Thorin raced forward and caught her, pulling her up against his chest.

"I don't think I can walk," she said matter-of-factly.

"I will carry you." He pulled her closer. Even though she had a curvy body, she was so tiny, so small, and so fragile.

Something stirred inside him. Something he hadn't felt for a very long time. His jaw clenched. He stared down at his large, scarred hands against her pale skin. They looked wrong against her smoothness.

Suddenly, her eyes widened. "Look out!"

Thorin automatically took a step backward. He saw the injured Thraxian guard rushing at them, blood gushing from a head wound.

He felt fingers at his belt. The female grabbed his dagger and reared up. She jammed the blade into the Thraxian's chest.

The alien made a gurgling sound and fell backward.

The female sagged back against Thorin's chest, eyeing the bloody knife with horror.

Gently, he took it from her.

"I'm Regan," she said.

"Thorin."

"Nice to meet you. Can we get out of here, Thorin?"

He pulled her closer, strange protective instincts flaring to life inside of him. "Yes."

And then he heard Raiden's roar. Thorin looked over and saw Harper slumped on the ground, writhing in pain. A big, scarred Thraxian was standing over her, his staff raised ominously.

"Harper," Regan said, her voice frightened.

Thorin watched, as Raiden sprinted, leaping over dead bodies. He rammed his sword into the Thraxian.

***

Raiden thrust his sword deeper into the Thraxian's worthless body. Then he wrenched it free, not even watching as the alien fell.

Raiden fell to his knees beside Harper. "Harper."

She tried to move, but fell back, her face pale. "I think I'm going to pass out. Hurts."

He ran a shaking hand over her cheek. "It's okay. I've got you."

She looked up at him, her gaze a little unfocused. "I'm glad you came back."

He pulled her into his arms, hating when she cried out. She had broken bones and needed the healers. She bit her lip and slumped against his chest, unconscious.

He looked to the others. Lore looked even more battered, but he was on his feet and Nero was helping him. Thorin was cradling Harper's friend, Regan. She looked tiny in the big man's arms. "Let's get back to safety."

As they raced out of the ship, Thorin moved up beside him.

Raiden looked at Regan. "She okay?"

"She has a name," the woman said, in a quiet but annoyed voice.

Raiden felt a smile threatening. Apparently the

females of Earth had a few things in common. "Sorry. Regan. I'm glad you're okay."

"She'd already got herself free of the restraints," Thorin said in a bemused tone.

"How's Harper?" Regan asked.

"Hurt. She's passed out from the pain."

"She'll be fine once we get her to a regen tank to heal." Thorin's gaze went to Raiden's. "The commander?"

"He got away." Raiden shook his head. "It doesn't matter."

And it didn't. Nothing mattered right now, except that the woman he loved was hurt. His arms tightened on her at the realization. He loved her. *Loved her*? He searched his feelings, knowing without a doubt what he felt was real. He couldn't lose her.

Thankfully, they avoided meeting any other Thraxians, and it wasn't long before they stepped out of the ship and into the night air.

But as they moved away from the shadow of the Thraxian ship, big shapes came out of the darkness.

His gut cramped. The commander and a fresh set of guards.

Drak. Raiden cursed. They were injured, tired, and they had Harper and Regan to protect. Raiden ran through every option in his head, trying to find a way out.

"Give the women to us," the commander said. "I plan to sell them to the worst slavers I can find." His gaze bored into Raiden. "And you will finally die like the rest of your planet."

Raiden was willing to give his life to protect Harper. He traded a glance with Thorin. "Ready for another fight?"

Thorin nodded. "I'm always ready for another fight."

Suddenly, shouts broke out from the back of the group of Thraxians.

Raiden tensed, then saw the group part, each one going for their weapons.

Galen, Saff, and Kace rushed into the fray, swinging their weapons. Galen was a deadly force, fighting with a double-bladed sword.

Raiden took a brief moment to watch the man in action. The man could own the arena, if he'd fight. He'd taught Raiden everything he knew.

Yoxx ran.

Galen leaped on him, taking him down. The commander bucked beneath Galen's boots.

Raiden tensed, but simply tightened his hold on the woman in his arms. Galen met his gaze, a question in his eyes. His face looked as though it had been carved from rock. He'd lost everything, too, when Aurelia had fallen.

Raiden nodded.

Galen landed the killing blow.

As the remaining Thraxians realized their commander lay on the dirt, defeated, they broke away, running toward the Thraxian ship. The fight was over.

Raiden stepped closer, staring at the body of the alien he'd hated his entire life, and felt…nothing.

He met his friend's gaze. "Thanks for the backup." Galen nodded and Raiden hitched Harper's still form higher in his arms. "I need to get Harper to a regen tank."

***

Harper woke, floating in goo.

She wrinkled her nose. It was a strange feeling, like she was swimming in a pool of gelatin. She felt no pain. She gripped the sides of the regen tank and moved her legs. All healed.

She sat up, and gingerly pulled herself out of the tank. No one seemed to be around. She stood beside the tank, shivering, blue goo dripping off her and onto the floor.

Then she spotted the chair near her tank and the big gladiator fast asleep in it. Her heart clenched. He looked exhausted, his face drawn.

He'd come for her. Yeah, he'd screwed up, but in the end, he'd come for her. Her perfectly imperfect gladiator.

She grabbed a large drying cloth from a stack nearby and toweled herself dry. She spotted a silky robe tossed over the back of a second chair. Gripping the chair for balance, she pulled the robe around her body.

She moved over to Raiden, drinking in the sight of him.

Suddenly, his eyes opened. "Harper?" He reached out and pulled her toward him. He pressed his face into her belly. "You're okay?"

"All healed." She ran her hands over his short hair. "How's Regan?"

"Fine. Resting. She's a little rattled, but strangely, Thorin has been very protective. I wasn't sure if his hovering was helping or hindering, but Regan seems to find him comforting."

Big, bad Thorin comforting? "I'm sure he means well."

"Yes, he does."

"And Rory?"

Raiden shook his head. "Galen is searching for her and waiting to hear from his contacts."

"Dammit." Harper pulled in a shaky breath. *I'm so sorry, Rory.*

"We'll find her."

Harper nodded. "Rory is tough and she's also had years of training in mixed martial arts...hand-to-hand combat. But she also has a quick temper. She'll push, and prod, and fight." Which would get the engineer hurt. "I won't give up until we find her, and Madeline Cochran. She was taken as well." Harper prayed Madeline was on Carthago.

Raiden looked up at Harper. "I'm sorry."

She frowned. "For what? Rory? Saving me? For getting me out of there and healing me?"

"You would have saved yourself." He looked up at her. "I'm sorry for being an ass, and leaving you in the first place."

"I'm just glad you came back." She let her gaze drift down his hard, tattooed body. He was hers. All hers. "Why did you?"

"You were right," he said. "Revenge is...empty. I

heard you were in trouble and realized killing the commander gained me nothing. Losing you would destroy everything I had."

She leaned down and pressed her lips gently against his.

His hand gripped her jaw. "You fill me up, Harper. You fill up all the dark, empty spaces."

She felt a warmth bloom in her chest. "Nice words, gladiator."

"I was empty for a long time. A part of me was locked down after I lost my family and world. I'm not empty anymore."

He reached up, his callused hands pushing the robe off her shoulders. She thought he was going to pull her into his lap, but instead, his hands moved over her limbs. He checked her arms, cupped her breasts, probed her ribs. Then his hands slid down her belly, leaving a trail of heated sensation in their wake.

He smoothed his way down her legs, pausing at the places she knew Scar Face had broken.

"I'm all healed, Raiden."

"I needed to check for myself." Now, he yanked her into his lap.

She straddled him, feeling his hard cock beneath her. "Someone might come in."

"I locked the door." He tore open his trousers.

She moved against him. "So, are you going to tell me how you feel about me?"

"I told you. I feel everything for you."

"Raiden. That's not what I want to hear."

"A gladiator isn't supposed to talk about feelings."

She moved again, teasing him. "So gladiators are afraid of something."

"Gladiators are not afraid."

"Hah, got you. Fear is a feeling."

He smiled, cupping her jaw again. "With you, I feel pleasure, joy, annoyance, fear." He shifted her hips, the thick head of his cock rubbed against her slick center.

She moaned. "What else, Raiden?"

"Love." He pushed inside her, so impossibly slowly. "I love you, my little gladiator of Earth."

She gasped, gripping his shoulders. "I love you, too, Raiden. And I'm not little."

"You are to me."

She slid one hand up to cup his stubbled cheek. "No one's ever really loved me. Not enough to keep me."

He growled. "Mine." He started to move her hips faster, his own hips plunging up. "You're mine, Harper. I'm keeping you, and I'm never letting you go."

"Always," she answered.

They kept moving against each other, him stretching her and filling her in a way no one ever had before. "Harder," she murmured. "Faster."

"No."

Frustratingly, he slowed down. His hand slid down between their bodies, over her quivering belly, finding the slick little nub of her clit.

They moved together, the room filled with their

husky cries and murmurs. As he started rubbing her in tight, little circles, her breath hitched.

His gaze locked with her. "This time, we go slow. Because we have forever."

***

Raiden wanted to take his time. He wanted to love Harper and not rush.

So much of their loving had been wild and wanton. Now, he wanted to show her something else.

As he filled her, thrusting slowly in and out of her body, he watched the emotions washing over her face. He would never get tired of watching them. And the one that he could see most was love.

He'd never felt like he deserved love before. Now, he was never going to let it go.

Moments later she came, her head dropping back, her body squeezing down on his cock. As she cried his name, he felt his own release threatening, and he felt a shining instant where there was nothing bad, or ugly. Oh, it would be back—that was life and she was a capricious mistress at times—but right now, she was beautiful, and joyous, and full of wonder.

He gripped Harper's hips, pulling her down, and shoved himself deep. He held himself there, trying not to shout as he poured himself inside her.

When he could finally make sense of his thoughts, she was kissing his neck and jaw. She curled up in his lap, holding on tight.

Suddenly, the door slammed open and gladiators poured in.

Harper let out a squeak. "You said you locked it!"

"I did." Someone had picked the lock. He suspected Lore's tricky fingers.

"Oh, my God." Harper's horrified whisper brushed against Raiden's ear. "You're still *inside* me."

Raiden reached down and grabbed her discarded robe, pulling it over her body. It covered...most of her.

"She okay?"

"How's she feeling?"

Thorin gave an amused snort. "Oh, she looks perfectly fine to me."

"She's healed," Raiden told his friends. "She's fine."

She smiled at him. "Very fine."

There were bawdy chuckles all around. Harper groaned and buried her face in his neck.

"Sure you want to tie yourself to me and this rowdy lot?"

She looked up at him. "Yes, Raiden. Forever."

Chapter Twenty

Showered and dressed, Harper headed to see Regan.

Galen had given her a private room not far from the gladiators' living area. She entered the light-filled space which was far smaller and tidier than Raiden's room.

Regan looked clean and rested and much better than the last time Harper had seen her. She was sitting on a bench, eating some strange purple fruit.

Harper cleared her throat. "Hi."

"Harper!" Regan rushed over and threw her arms around Harper.

Tears pricked at Harper's eyes. The feel of Regan's curvy form was familiar, and Harper hugged the woman back hard.

"You're okay?" Harper asked.

Regan pulled back and nodded. "Yes. Thanks to you." Then her friend frowned. "But you were hurt."

"I'm fine now. All healed. They have some pretty advanced medical technology. Don't let the stone architecture and the swords fool you."

"Rory?" Regan's eyes had a haunted look.

Harper squeezed her hands. "We're looking. We'll find her."

Regan squeezed her eyes shut, a sob catching in her chest. "God." Then, she swiped a hand at her face. "We'll find her. We won't stop until she's safe."

Harper nodded. "And Madeline, as well. It's a promise."

"And then what? How do we get home?" Regan chewed on her bottom lip. "Can we find a ship?"

Harper drew in a deep breath. "Sit down." She found herself sitting on the edge of a couch as her friend sat beside her.

Regan looked her in the eye. "They won't let us go, will they?"

Where the hell did she start? God, she hated to be the one to break the news to her.

"You can leave anytime you choose." Raiden's deep voice.

Harper looked over and saw him in the doorway. She smiled at him. The damn gladiator was here to support her. He strode over and stood behind her couch, resting his hand on her shoulder.

"This is Raiden. He's..." She wasn't quite sure how to describe him. Boyfriend sounded too juvenile. Lover?

"Hers. I'm hers."

"You're...you're *sleeping* with one of them?" Regan's voice was filled with shock.

She stared straight at her friend. "No, I fell in love with a loyal, brave man."

Regan sank back into the couch. "And we can

just leave? He's not holding you here against your will?"

"Of course he isn't. And yes, you can leave."

"You can go wherever you choose," Raiden added.

"Home," Regan said. "I want to go home.

Harper felt a hollow feeling creeping in. "It isn't quite that simple. The Thraxians who snatched us...they followed a random wormhole to reach our solar system. Earth is on the other side of the galaxy to Carthago."

There was a hushed silence.

"So we take the wormhole back," Regan said, watching Harper intently.

Harper drew breath. "It's closed. It no longer exists."

"So we find the ship and we take the long ride home," Regan said, her tone frantic.

Harper bit her lip "Even with the fastest spaceship, that will take roughly two hundred years."

Regan started shaking her head.

Harper gripped her friend's hands. "Everyone you know would be long dead."

"No."

"I'm sorry, there is no way back to Earth."

Regan pressed her lips together, pulling in some deep breaths. "I'm probably going to have a big fat breakdown about this later."

There was her steady scientist friend. Regan rarely fell apart. "You'll be entitled."

"You don't seem too upset about this," Regan said.

There was no judgment in Regan's tone, just curiosity. Harper gave a small nod. "I've had longer to process it. More time to come to terms with it. And there was nothing, no one, left for me on Earth, anyway."

She felt Raiden's fingers tighten on her shoulder. She looked up and smiled at him.

"I decided I could survive, give up, or thrive. I've made my choice." And it was the gladiator standing beside her. She looked back at her friend. "It's your choice, now."

"You have a place here at the House of Galen, if you choose," Raiden added.

Regan just watched them with sadness on her face. Harper vowed then and there to do whatever she had to do to ensure her friend found happiness.

***

"Raiden, I'm glad I caught you."

Raiden turned and saw Galen striding toward him. "G. You caught me before I headed out."

Galen thrust his hands on his hips. "I'm hearing rumblings that the Thraxians are out for revenge after our little…altercation."

Raiden gave a careless shrug. "That's nothing new. They can try, and we will beat them, as we always have."

Galen tilted his head. "You have something valuable to lose now."

Raiden grinned. "And she can take care of herself."

Galen gave him an answering smile. "So she can. I'm happy for you. I'm happy that you're happy."

Raiden grabbed his friend's arm. "You should give it a try."

Galen raised a brow. "A woman? Oh, no. I don't think so. They are far more trouble than they're worth."

"I'm going to ask her to let me put my mark on her."

Beneath his long sleeves, Galen carried Aurelian tattoos too. They were a tradition to capture stories, promises, and oaths. For a long time, Raiden had ignored the markings on his body while Galen had hidden his.

But now, loving Harper had helped something settle in Raiden. Now he wanted to celebrate his history and see his name on the skin of the woman he loved.

Galen went still. "She agreed?"

"I haven't asked her yet, but I've lined up the skin artist in the market if she says yes." Raiden imagined holding her as his name and the Aurelian markings of his family were etched on her skin.

After Raiden had left his friend, he went looking for his woman.

Thorin had mentioned she'd gone to the market to find some things for Regan. Raiden had a suspicion where he'd find her. As he moved through the streets, he knew that she was still hurting for her friend. She'd found a place where she was happy, but Regan was still walking around looking a little shell-shocked. And he knew they were both worried about the other women, Rory and Madeline. There had been no sign of the Earth women.

He took the ramp down to the market and soon reached the door to his pool. When he stepped out onto the tiles, he saw her form silhouetted against pool lights.

Her hair was wet, a drying sheet wrapped around her damp body.

From his woman's hunched shoulders, he could tell she was sad. He came up behind her and wrapped his arms around her.

"She just needs some time," he said.

Harper nodded. "I know. But unlike me, Regan has friends and family on Earth. And she can never go back. It will be harder for her." Harper turned in his arms. "She doesn't have a big, strong gladiator to lean on."

"We'll be there for her. And Rory and Madeline, when we find them."

Harper smiled. "My big, tough gladiator. You're just a big softie under that tough exterior."

With a growl, he leaned down and nipped at her lips. "You're going to get yourself challenged for talk like that. I have a reputation to uphold."

"Bring it on, gladiator."

He was glad to hear the humor in her voice, and to see the happiness dancing in her eyes. "You don't want me to challenge you. I'm bigger, stronger, and you'll never—"

She lashed out with a leg, and took him down. As he landed flat on his back, she came down on top of him, her knees jammed into his sides.

Yeah, he knew his woman well.

He rolled, and together they wrestled across the tiles, knocking over some plants. She fought back with all her strength, and he grunted as her fist landed in his gut. His little gladiator wasn't pulling her punches.

As they rolled again, he pinned her to the ground, listening to her laughter.

Yeah, Raiden had found his perfect match in every way.

"Harper, I want to ask you something."

She stilled. "It's important?"

He nodded, pulling her up so she was sitting in his lap. "I wanted to ask if you'd do me the honor of accepting my mark." He brushed his fingers up her arm. "Of letting me place our story and our commitment on your skin."

"Tattoos? Like yours."

He nodded. "It is an Aurelian tradition."

She smiled. "I love your ink, Raiden. I'd be honored." Her nose wrinkled. "It's going to hurt, isn't it?"

"There is a talented artist here in the market. I trust her. And I'll hold your hand, little gladiator."

She pushed him backward, climbing on top of him, knees digging into his chest. "You'll owe me. I want my name on your skin."

He'd already planned that. "Done." He wondered

if Harper realized he'd do anything for her.

She leaned down, her lips brushing his. "I really do love you. Gladiator, prince, man...you're all of those things to me."

"Gladiator, lover, and my heart. You're all those things to me."

"Pretty words for a tough, alpha-male gladiator." She rolled them so he was on top. "Now, how about you show me how much you love me?"

Raiden pressed his mouth to hers, pulling her close. Love and desire stormed through him. He'd spend the rest of his life ensuring his little gladiator knew just how much she was loved.

I hope you enjoyed Raiden and Harper's story! Galactic Gladiators continues with WARRIOR, the story of big, wild gladiator Thorin. Read on for a preview of the first chapter.

Don't miss out! For updates about new releases, action romance info, free books, and other fun stuff, sign up for my VIP mailing list and get your *free box set* containing three action-packed romances.

Visit here to get started:
www.annahackettbooks.com

FREE BOX SET DOWNLOAD

JOIN THE ACTION-PACKED ADVENTURE!

Formats: Kindle, ePub, PDF

Preview: Warrior

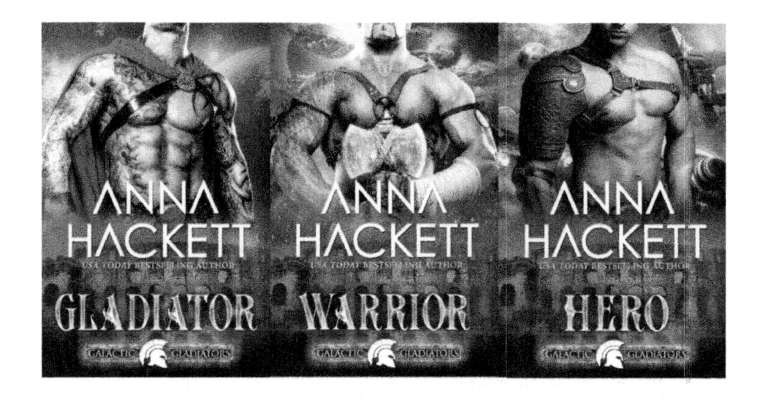

The roar of the crowd was electrifying.

Regan Forrest felt the hairs on her arms rise. She could feel the excitement and energy pumping off the crowd sitting in the stands around her. Some people were chanting, others were shouting out the names of their favorite gladiators, waiting for the fight to begin.

As she scanned the huge, old stone arena, she could almost imagine she was sitting back in the Colosseum in Ancient Rome. But then she blinked, and saw the different alien species sitting on the tiered seats. She heard the roar of engines, as a giant starship shot overhead, taking off from the nearby spaceport.

No, she was nowhere near Earth.

Instead, she'd been abducted by alien slavers

and transported to the other side of the galaxy.

The warm cream stone of the Kor Magna Arena might be old and worn through hundreds of years of gladiatorial fights, but around her, people were holding high-tech devices: communicators, binoculars, and who knew what else. Most of the technology wouldn't have looked out of place on the space station where she worked.

Correction. Where she *had* worked. She swallowed, her throat tightening. The Fortuna Space Station orbiting Jupiter probably didn't even exist anymore after the Thraxians had attacked it. Regan still couldn't believe that she'd gone from botanist to slave in the blink of an eye.

You're free now, Regan. She stared up. Free, but still light years from Earth, with no way to get home. She blinked as bright strobe lights hit her eyes. The arena's lights were coming on, even though the sun hadn't quite set. *Correction.* Suns. She watched the huge dual suns of Kor Magna sinking over the walls of the arena, heading toward the horizon of the desert planet.

Everything closed in on her. The noise thundered in her head, disorienting her. Her heart raced, and she shifted in her seat, trying to find some calm. The Thraxians had kept her locked up in a cell on their ship for so long, that now, sitting here surrounded by thousands of screaming people was too much. She felt a trickle of sweat roll down her spine, and once again, she looked up at the sky. But the two giant suns just reminded her that she wasn't on Earth and never would be again.

"Are you okay, Regan?"

The voice beside her instantly made the pressure in her head ease. She smiled at her friend Harper and reminded herself that no matter how bad things seemed, she wasn't alone. "Getting there." She nodded toward the stands. "This is pretty crazy, isn't it?"

Her friend smiled and bumped her shoulder against Regan's. "It's insane. But you'll get used to it." Harper's eagle-eyed gaze moved back down to the sand-covered floor of the arena, anticipation on her face. "The fights can be brutal, but there is no doubt that they're also amazing."

Regan managed a nod. Harper was her best friend, and the space marine had also been snatched off the space station. But while Regan was still trying to put on the weight she'd lost in captivity and negotiate this strange new world, Harper looked...great.

With her tall, athletic body and sleek, dark hair, Harper was glowing. She wore dark-leather pants and a leather vest that showed off her toned arms, as well as the gorgeous alien tattoos on her left one.

A symbol that one of the big, tough gladiators who was about to step into the arena had claimed her.

Regan still couldn't quite believe her friend had fallen in love with an alien gladiator, but she couldn't dispute the fact that Harper had found a place here in Kor Magna. She'd found a home, a place in the arena, and love. She wasn't just surviving, she was thriving.

And perhaps Regan could, as well.

She shifted in her seat again. Maybe. Galen, the Imperator of the House of Galen, had taken her in when Harper and his gladiators had rescued her. The intimidating man was in charge of everything to do with his House. He'd given her a room to stay in, and recently, another small space where she'd set up a small lab. She'd been going crazy doing nothing, and unlike Harper, who was trained in security and fighting, Regan couldn't even hold a sword, let alone fight in the arena.

Analyzing some of the fascinating alien substances she'd come across was keeping her sane. Her lab was her own little oasis in the midst of chaos.

For a brief second, she thought of her parents back on Earth. Did they miss her? Were they grieving for her? Pain seared her heart. No, probably not. Her parents had disowned her long before she'd been abducted.

The cries of the crowd rose to deafening levels. Around them, lots of people leaped to their feet, waving their hands in the air.

"Here they come," Harper said.

They were sitting in the seats assigned to the House of Galen, right up close to the arena floor. Regan had a perfect view as the gladiators entered.

She felt a lick of excitement. She knew exactly who she was waiting to see.

Saff strode in first. The female gladiator had it all—muscled body, glossy dark skin, and black hair pulled back in an abundance of braids. She raised an arm above her head, waving at the crowd. In her other hand, she was holding something small. Regan knew Saff's weapon of choice was a special kind of net, as well as the short sword attached to her belt.

The House of Galen's gladiators all worked in pairs, and Saff's partner followed her in. Kace was about as clean-cut as a gladiator got, with bronze skin and a detailed, leather arm guard over his right shoulder and muscled bicep. He had a handsome, hard-planed face. He nodded to the crowd, his long metal staff held in one strong hand.

Another pair of gladiators stepped out onto the sand. Regan didn't know these two as well, but both were tall. Lore was far leaner, with a long fall of tawny hair, while his partner, Nero, was a huge mountain of a gladiator. Lore turned in a circle and threw something in the air. A small cloud of smoke rose up, before fireworks shot up into the sky.

The crowd cheered and Nero scowled.

Lore was an illusionist, and used his tricks to charm the crowd. He'd told Regan that everything that happened in the arena was just one big show.

Then, the final pair of House of Galen gladiators stepped out of the tunnel and entered the arena. The roar of the crowd exploded.

Beside Regan, Harper let out a sharp whistle. Regan looked at Raiden first. Every tattooed, hard inch of him. He wore simple leather straps across his chest, which were attached to a blood-red cloak that fell down his back. Tattoos in black ink covered his arms and chest. He was an imposing sight, champion of the arena, and loved by all the spectators. He didn't even glance at the crowd. He was there to fight.

Then Regan saw *him*.

Raiden's partner was a huge warrior called Thorin.

Big, broad shoulders and a hard chest crisscrossed with dark leather. He was all corded muscle, and his rugged face was set off by his shaved head. He smiled for the crowd, lifting a huge axe up in one hand.

He had big hands. Rough hands. She'd studied those hands closely when he'd carried her off the Thraxian slave ship. And she'd studied them a lot over the last few weeks, as she'd settled in at the House of Galen.

Thorin played to the crowd, turning in a slow circle. She took in the back view of him. Dark-brown leather trousers clung to him. The man had a magnificent ass and legs like tree trunks. He was just so masculine, rugged, and a little wild. He fascinated her.

Regan shifted in her seat. After two weeks in the House of Galen, she knew she was safe. She was no longer stuck in a cell, starving, or being beaten. She felt like she was waking up from a nightmare, slowly coming back to life.

Looking at Thorin made something else inside her come back to life, too.

He finished his circle and stopped. That was when she realized he was looking at her.

As their gazes connected, Regan felt a zip of

electricity race through her. She lifted a hand in greeting.

He gave her one short nod before he turned to join the other gladiators.

Regan let out a shaky breath. She was a sensible scientist, and she'd been raised by strict parents who were always concerned with what the neighbors thought. Never in her entire life had Regan felt the urge to climb a man's huge, muscled body and wrap her legs around his waist, but she did now. Boy, did she ever.

The voices of the announcers echoed through the arena, and thanks to the language translator device the Thraxians had implanted in her head, she had no trouble understanding their words.

The competitors had entered the arena.

As she saw the opposing gladiators come out of the tunnel on the opposite side of the arena, her muscles locked tight.

Tonight, the House of Galen were fighting their bitter rivals—the House of Thrax.

The same aliens who had abducted Regan and Harper, and however many others from Fortuna. Her hands twisted together. She knew her cousin Rory, an engineer on the space station, was here, somewhere. She'd been a prisoner of the Thraxians but had been moved before she could be rescued.

We'll find you, Rory. I promise. Harper had also seen the civilian commander of the space station, Madeline Cochran, get snatched too. But so far, despite the best efforts of the House of Galen gladiators, there had been no sign of the women.

Regan tried to pull a breath into her constricted lungs. Her gaze zeroed in on the gladiators below. Not all the gladiators for the House of Thrax were Thraxians, but a few were. She easily picked them out. They looked like the demons they were. Massive bodies covered in toughened, dark-brown skin, a set of sharp horns that protruded from the top of their heads, and small tusks on either side of their mouths. Even from this distance, she saw the faint glow of orange veins under their skin.

For a second, the arena swam, and Regan was back in her cell. Her stomach turned over, and she thought she might be sick. Then she blinked, and saw Thorin watching her again. As her gaze flicked to the Thraxian gladiators and then back to him, she saw his face harden.

The Thraxians worshipped strength and might above all else, and they saw nothing wrong with being cruel to those beneath them. As a small, puny woman from a backward planet like Earth, they'd seen her as no better than an ant. Completely worthless.

Harper leaned forward. "The fight's about to begin."

A siren sounded deafeningly—the long, mournful wail of a horn.

The House of Thrax gladiators charged forward, roaring battle cries. The House of Galen gladiators spread out a little, their feet shoulder width apart, holding their weapons easily, like natural extensions of their bodies.

Regan watched the gladiators clash together.

Raiden, Thorin, and the others hit hard. There were no soft blows, just bone-rattling hit after hit, and soon, she saw gladiators stumbling, and blood splattering on the sand.

She pressed a hand to her tight stomach. She reminded herself that this wasn't a fight to the death. Here in Kor Magna, the gladiator houses spent a small fortune purchasing, training, and caring for their gladiators. They made a lot of money in the arena and from corporate sponsorship, so losing a gladiator was bad all around.

But that didn't mean there weren't a lot of injuries—bad ones. Harper had told her that the houses also spent a lot of money on medical technology to ensure the gladiators could be patched up after each fight.

She watched as Thorin swung his axe. They'd be fine. All of them. She knew they'd been fighting in the arena for a very long time.

Thorin took down one of the Thraxians. He charged past the throng of fighters, and then spotted a smaller, frightened gladiator. The young man had a long, narrow build and was holding an axe that looked far too heavy for him. He was shaking in terror.

Thorin gripped the man's arm and pushed him toward Raiden. Raiden said something and then pushed the man back behind the House of Galen gladiators. The smaller man fell into the sand, crying.

This was another reason Regan felt so safe at

the House of Galen. These big, tough fighters also had the need to protect in their bones. Harper had told her they made it their mission to clandestinely help weaker fighters who ended up in the arena.

Thorin charged a larger, taller gladiator. His axe slammed against the sword of the big fighter, shattering it. She watched, mesmerized, as he plowed through his opponents.

That's when she realized he was targeting only the gladiators who were of the Thraxian species. Her breath hitched. He was taking down each gladiator who was of the species who'd stolen and abused her. She pressed a fist to her chest, feeling her heart knocking against her ribs.

No one had ever fought for her before.

A second Thraxian came in from the side, out of Thorin's line of sight. She leaped to her feet without realizing, and when the crowd cried out, Regan did as well.

The sword had cut into Thorin's shoulder. She gripped the rail. Blood flowed down his chest and bicep.

"It's not bad," a deep voice said from behind her.

That low, gravelly voice made her glance over her shoulder. She hadn't noticed Galen arrive.

The Imperator of the House of Galen was a few years older than his gladiators, but still in fighting shape. He had a hard, muscled body, a scarred face, and an eye patch over one eye. His remaining eye was a brilliant, icy blue. His dark hair was brushed back off his imposing face, and had a few strands of gray at the temples.

"It takes more than a cut to take Thorin down," Harper said from beside her.

Regan nodded, but she gripped the railing so tightly her knuckles started to turn white. When she turned back to the fight, she saw that they were right. Thorin continued fighting like he hadn't been hurt. It didn't even slow him down.

He threw his axe, and she watched it slam into the large shield of one of his opponents. The shield cracked down the middle. The crowd went wild, and as she saw Thorin scoop up his axe and turn to attack again, she felt the energy of the fight fill her. A part of her was excited. By the cheering crowd, by the primal fighting, by Thorin's focus and prowess.

She understood why places like the Kor Magna Arena existed. Why fights like this appealed to the crowd and drew spectators from all over the galaxy. For the duration of the fight, everyone in the stands could be connected to the wild, primal part of their nature. As a scientist, she knew it existed. The fight spoke to the parts of a person that had been honed in the past. The fight-or-flight instinct every creature had.

For the duration of the fight, every person could forget about the mundane and stressful parts of their lives, and just focus on the raw battle of survival.

With a final clash of metal on metal, the fight was over.

As the announcers cried out the name of the House of Galen, the crowd was on its feet, cheering.

Regan watched as medical teams rushed forward to collect the injured and writhing Thraxian gladiators from the sand.

Harper leaned forward. "Maybe Thorin's injury was worse than we thought."

Regan saw Thorin was bleeding badly. His entire chest was covered with blood. Worried, she jumped up. "We need to help him."

Harper shot her a look. "Galen's got an entire medical team—"

But Regan was already hurrying to get to the entrance to the tunnels to meet the winning gladiators.

She'd been playing around with the fantastic med gel the Medical team used, trying to enhance its properties. It could help Thorin.

And, for some reason, she wouldn't believe Thorin was all right until she saw it with her own eyes.

Galactic Gladiators

Gladiator

Warrior

Hero

Also by Anna Hackett

Treasure Hunter Security

Undiscovered

Uncharted

Unexplored

Galactic Gladiators

Gladiator

Warrior

Hero

Hell Squad

Marcus

Cruz

Gabe

Reed

Roth

Noah

Shaw

Holmes

Niko

Finn

The Anomaly Series

Time Thief

Mind Raider

Soul Stealer

Salvation

Anomaly Series Box Set

The Phoenix Adventures

Among Galactic Ruins

At Star's End

In the Devil's Nebula

On a Rogue Planet

Beneath a Trojan Moon

Beyond Galaxy's Edge

On a Cyborg Planet

Return to Dark Earth

On a Barbarian World

Lost in Barbarian Space

Through Uncharted Space

Perma Series

Winter Fusion

The WindKeepers Series

Wind Kissed, Fire Bound

Taken by the South Wind

Tempting the West Wind

Defying the North Wind

Claiming the East Wind

Standalone Titles

Savage Dragon

Hunter's Surrender

One Night with the Wolf

Anthologies

A Galactic Holiday

Moonlight (UK only)

Vampire Hunter (UK only)

Awakening the Dragon (UK Only)

For more information visit AnnaHackettBooks.com

About the Author

I'm a USA Today bestselling author and I'm passionate about ***action romance***. I love stories that combine the thrill of falling in love with the excitement of action, danger and adventure. I'm a sucker for that moment when the team is walking in slow motion, shoulder-to-shoulder heading off into battle.

I write about people overcoming unbeatable odds and achieving seemingly impossible goals. I like to believe it's possible for all of us to do the same.

My books are mixture of action, adventure and sexy romance and they're recommended for anyone who enjoys fast-paced stories where the boy wins the girl at the end (or sometimes the girl wins the boy!)

For release dates, action romance info, free books, and other fun stuff, sign up for the latest news here:

Website: AnnaHackettBooks.com

Printed in Great Britain
by Amazon